KUMAKHA
WARRIOR QUEEN

An Historical Fiction Novel

GEORGE PA DOVER

OP Books is an imprint of Olai Press, a division of Olai Multiversal Enterprises LLC.
27137 Nudgent Street
Boron, CA 93516

Olai Press, OP Books, WD Books, Blossom Books, and their logos are trademarks of Olai Multiversal Enterprises LLC.

Dover, George P A, 1960 –
Kumakha Warrior Queen / George P A Dover. 1st OP Books ed.
p. cm
ISBN: 978-0-9818503-6 (alk. Paper)

    1.   Pre-slavery Alkebulan — Fiction
    2.   Kumasi, Ghana — Fiction
    3.   Genetic Memory — Fiction
    4.   Alkebulan Spiritualism — Fiction
    5.   Trans-Atlantic Slave Trade — Fiction
    6.   Dutch & British Guiana — Fiction
    7.   Rebellion & Survival
I. Title
Cover illustration done by Kofi Jah G on Canva

Manufactured in the United States of America

PART ONE

The wisdom of a queen isn't born from privilege — it's forged in the fires of experience. Every challenge faced, every obstacle overcome, adds another layer to her understanding of the world and her place within it.

--Source unknown

FOREWORD

I write these words not as an author inventing, but as a descendant remembering. What you hold in your hands is no ordinary book. It is a relic, drawn from the earth of my own backyard, where for centuries it had rested beneath black sage trees until the ancestors deemed the time right for me to unearth it. Bound in wood, written in a script both delicate and commanding, the manuscript revealed itself to me as *Edna the Warrior Queen of Kumakha: 1713–1798.*

At first, I thought I had simply found a hidden treasure of history. But as I flipped through the delicate pages, reading the hand-written words, the voice of Edna, familiar, insistent, undeniable, stirred within me. Her struggles, her triumphs, her visions were not foreign; they pulsed through my own blood. Soon, I understood why: I am her descendant, the eleventh generation born of her defiance. This story is mine as much as it is hers, though it is she who forged it in blood, fire, and faith. And so, I retell her life in multiple narrative voices, including the omniscient, not to replace her own, but to illuminate it for the living; to ensure her dagger still gleams, her spirit still walks, her commands and her fury still echo among us more than four hundred years later.

ONE

When Vernon Byrne first noticed the dirt mound while clearing bushes at the back end of the house lot he and his wife, Rowena, had recently purchased in Kumakha Village, on the East Bank of Demerara in British Guiana, he furrowed his brow into tight lines. *An ant nest?* he wondered. Using his tree-limb hook—"a fork," as Guyanese call it— he pulled back a cluster of black sage trees and ran his eyes along the length of the mound. *Hmm!* He estimated it to be about six feet long, between two and three and a half feet wide, and roughly a foot and a half high. *I've never seen an ant nest this big before,* he silently told himself. Letting the cluster of trees go, he began trampling the surrounding shrubs to see if there were other mounds. He slashed and stamped down a good ten square feet but found none. The raised, symmetrical ground was inconsistent with the topography of the area. Though Vernon had not been born and raised in Kumakha, he was no stranger to its cultural and physical character. He had spent most of his school holidays there — playing ketchup, roaming, and hunting with his cousins.

The village legend passed down to his generation placed the burial ground squarely at the center of Kumakha, where his ancestors had begun settling. With their strict adherence to Alkebulan traditions, they were unlikely to have deviated from customary burial rituals. But then he remembered what Aunt Drusilla had told him on the day he purchased the lot: that it was "virgin land." With that in mind, he pushed all conjecture aside and returned to his task.

He cleared the rest of the backyard but left the cluster of black sage trees intact, directly surrounding and on top of the mound. He then stacked the cut grass around the cluster, to be used later as mulch. Black sage berries were edible and highly nutritious, so he resolved to nurture the trees and encourage his children to do the same in the years ahead. *I'm sure they'll enjoy eating the berries someday,* Vernon thought. He had no inkling that eighteen years later, his only son, Michael, would uncover within that mound an epic story reaching back eleven generations — into eighteenth-century West Alkebulan, at the height of the Ashanti Kingdom and the zenith of the Trans-Atlantic Slave Trade.

Vernon and Rowena had worked long hours together—sometimes day and night, as time and resources allowed—building their house from scratch. They made a great couple, complementing each other in countless ways, and both understood that their success depended on mutual respect, teamwork, harmony, and clear communication. They committed to their roles in building the family, never stepping across each other's boundaries.

By 1959—five years after breaking ground—they had completed most of the construction to their great satisfaction. Three months later, their second child, Michael, was born. The industrious couple had much to celebrate, especially Rowena, whose life before meeting Vernon had been marred by selfishness, tragedy, hatred, and economic hardship. She had slid from the echelons of the upper class down to the struggling proletarian class.

TWO

By the time she turned eighteen, Rowena Daniels had already grown into a head-turning, jaw-dropping young woman who could make men walk into or stumble over objects. Her shoulder-length hair was jet-black and shiny. Her facial features were symmetrical and proportionate, with the width of each eye equal to the distance between them, and her eyes themselves deep, mysterious. Physically, she embodied femininity, grace, and sensuality combined — and her medium chocolate-brown complexion only heightened her appeal.

But Rowena's allure extended beyond her beauty. Her socioeconomic standing placed her among the most sought-after young women of her generation. Fully aware of this, her father, Harold Daniels, more than her mother, Maudeline, was determined to secure the best, most qualified suitor for her.

Rowena came of age during the early to mid-1900s, when many families of Alkebulan descent in British Guiana — despite the inequities imposed by British-owned financial institutions — had climbed the socioeconomic ladder into the upper class. The Daniels family, who had established the first post office on the Essequibo Coast, belonged to this class, and they intended to ensure their two daughters remained securely within it. Love was not considered a prerequisite. As Harold often reminded them: *"Love wouldn't keep roofs over your heads, put food in your stomachs, or decent clothes on your backs."*

Though they did not agree, Rowena and her sister, Rosemarie, felt they had little choice but to comply. Such subservience was expected of young women of good social standing at the time.

Thus, over a special supper for Rowena's eighteenth birthday, Maudeline made a solemn announcement:

"Rowena dear, your father has something very important to say."

The formality of her mother's tone told Rowena that her parents had already discussed the matter and agreed to its terms. She glanced at Rosemarie, who, sitting opposite, knit her brows. Rowena took the gesture not as bewilderment but as a silent warning: *Uh oh! Are you ready for this?* The sisters, so alike they could have passed for twins, often communicated through subtle expressions. Together, they sat back, bracing themselves.

Harold wasted no time. "An upstanding and righteous family has moved into town recently, as I'm sure you both must have heard," he said. "They have a very ambitious and good-looking son, who is also very good with his hands. I know this last part for a fact because I've seen his work. I'd like you to meet him soon, Row."

Whenever he used the shortened form of his daughters' names, they knew he was in a good mood and inclined to show them his softer side. Harold was a man of few words, his actions usually aligning with his principles. Yet the lessons he preached would not always serve Rowena well in the years to come.

She looked at her mother, who sat opposite Harold, her eyes fixed on her plate. Out of the corner of her own eye, Rowena saw her father staring hard at Maudeline, as if silently commanding her not to object. Though neither parent ever spoke of their union, Rowena had heard whispers that their marriage, like most among upper- and middle-class Alkebulan families in the village—ninety-five percent, by rumor—had been arranged.

In 1917, when Rowena was born, Harold was twenty-six and Maudeline nineteen. Both had been born in the late 1800s, less than a century after emancipation. Among the well-to-do post-emancipation families, the prevailing mentality was to distance themselves as far as possible from the vestiges of slavery. Wealth—acquired through enterprise or intermarriage—was the surest vehicle.

Harold tapped his robust, calloused fingers on the polished mahogany table, breaking the silence that followed his announcement. Knowing she owed much to this hardworking man who had given her a life of comfort and status, Rowena reasoned the least she could do was uphold a tradition that would secure the same for his grandchildren. She cleared her throat, turned toward him, and asked, her voice steady:

"So when have you arranged for me to meet this 'good-looking' young man of whom you've spoken, my dear father?"

She then looked at her mother and sister. Maudeline smiled the way she always did when her daughters acted boldly—questionable, perhaps, but worthy of respect. Rosemarie did not smile back, only knitting her brows tighter.

"The Alleynes are expected to visit on Sunday— this coming Sunday—just before supper," Harold said, addressing them all before turning directly to Rowena. "I suggest you handle the cooking that day, Row, and prepare a sumptuous meal. As they say, the fastest way to a man's heart is through his stomach."

"Amen!" Maudeline said. Rosemarie rolled her eyes and stifled a chuckle.

"So it shall be," Rowena replied, rising from her seat. "May I be excused now?"

"Yes, you may," her father said with a nod.

Rowena retreated quietly to her bedroom. Closing the door softly behind her, she sat at her purpleheart vanity and wept—for she knew she had just conceded to an arrangement that demanded she sacrifice personal choice for familial obligation.

THREE

Three and a half years into her arranged marriage, Rowena — the young stay-at-home wife of a man fourteen years her senior and mother of two children — attended to her family duties with deft devotion. Free from outside employment, she put her culinary skills to excellent use in the kitchen. Her knowledge of home economics and other "necessities" (as her husband called them) grew steadily. She sewed clothes for herself and the children, stitched curtains for the windows and doorways, and crafted linens for the beds. Joseph, however, ordered his own clothes tailor-made, and he alone handled all the family's financial affairs. Not once had he ever placed money directly in Rowena's hands, except for groceries.

Joseph Alleyne and his parents, Walter and Katherine Alleyne, had immigrated from Barbados with a hefty sum inherited from Walter's British father, a former winery owner on the island. After both parents (Walter's mother of Alkebulan descent and his father white British) died in a boating accident off the Barbadian coast, Walter — an only child — sold the winery and moved with his family to British Guiana, then popularly known as "The Breadbasket of the Caribbean." They settled in Ana Regina on the Essequibo Coast.

From a young age, Joseph, like his father, learned to work with his hands. He began making barrels for his grandfather's winery, then turned his skill to furniture. With the abundance of exotic woods in Guiana and the financial means to purchase them, *Alleyne & Son Furniture Store* was quickly established and prospered. But tragedy soon unraveled its success.

While restoring an old Victorian China cabinet, Walter stepped on a rusty nail. He poured alcohol on the wound, assuming it would suffice, but the infection spread. By the time Joseph realized the danger, it was too late. Walter contracted tetanus, and the infection overtook his body. Grief-stricken, Katherine sought refuge in alcohol, lost her mind, and was eventually institutionalized.

As if *Alleyne & Son* had formed a pact with misfortune, tragedy struck again. While Rowena was pregnant with her third child — whom she and Joseph had hoped would be a girl — Joseph fell gravely ill. Doctors diagnosed a brain tumor, and by then it was too late. He had only six months to live, bedridden for them all.

One day, realizing his end was near, Joseph called Rowena to his side. He revealed where he had hidden the family money. Then, with little surprise to Rowena, he added coldly:

"Every day, from now on, I will tell you exactly what I want to eat, and you will go to the market to buy only that. Nothing else. And one more very important thing: make sure you take a plate for my mother every single day."

He coughed violently, his body convulsing, then composed himself and continued, his face rigid: "I will not leave a single penny of my hard-earned money for another man to spend." His words tore through Rowena like a blade. Dumbfounded, she stared at the man who had been forced upon her, now shrunk in his bed, his once-imposing frame reduced, his face withered, his eyes sunken. "I have nothing else to say," Joseph added, turning his face away.

Rowena stumbled from the room in a daze. She had always known hers was a loveless marriage to an insensitive man. But she had never imagined his selfishness would run so deep that he would sacrifice his children's welfare simply to gratify his pride. Until that moment, she had at least respected him as a provider. Now she felt only the heavy obligation of nursing him to his grave.

In the living room, she sat on the couch and called her sons. They came running, beaming with the carefree joy only children so young — three and two — could carry. She patted the cushions beside her.

"Sit down," she said softly. She longed to explain, to prepare them for what was coming. But how could toddlers understand? *Had she been schooled in the Romantic poets,* she might have thought of Wordsworth: *"A simple Child / That lightly draws its breath / And feels its life in every limb / What should it know of death?"* Yet there was no room for poetry in her world. What mattered was survival—figuring out how to provide for her children.

When the boys nestled against her, she wrapped them tightly in her arms, pressing them to her bulging stomach. In her heart she whispered: *Soon, there will be three of you, and God will show us the way.*

Over the next months, Rowena followed Joseph's instructions faithfully. Each day she went to the market to buy expensive cuts of steak, mutton, fish, even canned corned beef— whatever he requested. Each day she wondered what future awaited her once the money was gone. Joseph had leased a beautiful colonial-style house on a street behind the family store near the high bridge in Ana Regina. With little of her own savings—scraped together from her resourcefulness in home economics—she could not keep it. Employment opportunities for women were scarce, and with children, impossible. She could not return to her parents' home either; once married, a woman was considered her husband's responsibility, no matter the circumstances. Her father had reminded her of that "tradition" many times. Still, she held her head high. By day, she carried out his requests. By night, she cried silently so her boys would not see.

At last, the day came when she spent the final penny of Joseph's hidden money. That evening, he ate half a plate of sirloin pork, tenderloin steak, and shoulder mutton pepperpot. He burped, closed his eyes—and never opened them again.

FOUR

With the generous—and often clandestine—support of her mother and sister, along with whatever income she could earn through her home economics skills, Rowena managed to keep a roof over her children's heads, food in their stomachs, and clothes on their backs. Yet she often wondered why life had to be so difficult. Why would God bless her with three beautiful children, and a husband who, though she had not loved him, had at least provided abundantly for them—only to snatch that security away in the blink of an eye?

Growing up, Rowena had been an avid reader. In her early teens, thanks to her father's social connections, she had gained access to books on philosophy, religion, mysticism, and, most importantly to her, the history of Alkebulans before slavery. Until she was betrothed—and subsequently consumed by homemaking—she had read enough on these subjects to not only understand much about life but also to question it.

As she sat on a bus heading home from Suddie Hospital—where construction was underway on a new wing and where she had gone to seek permission to sell food to the laborers—her mind returned to something she had once read:

14

Nothing happens accidentally. Life unfolds like a chain reaction. Disruption, painful as it may be, comes only to usher in the next phase of one's journey.

Caught in the harsh reality of her present struggles, Rowena could not yet imagine what the next phase of her life would look like after such drastic change. Still, she felt an undeniable compulsion to act—like going to the hospital for permission, which she had successfully obtained—driven by pure intuition and a heightened sense of awareness. She recalled another truth she had encountered in her readings: that her ancestors had long mastered the art of intuition and the wisdom of acting upon it, centuries before the Transatlantic Slave Trade.

The indomitable queens and warrior women of those distant times only deepened Rowena's fascination. Though respectful of her family's traditions and much of the post-emancipation culture of her people—often sacrificing her own beliefs to uphold them—she always felt slightly out of place in her own time. Yes, she lived in the twentieth century in flesh and blood, but deep within, she sensed there was more to her being. Something was missing. Or perhaps, she was missing something.

In one book on philosophy, she had read about a hypothesis that memory could be encoded genetically—that human beings might pass down experiences, in all their sensory forms, to future generations. After reflecting on it, Rowena concluded that it made perfect sense. After all, were they not the extensions and continuations of their ancestors? Were they not, in truth, their ancestors manifested in different forms, in different times? She also remembered reading of the pharaohs, embalmed to preserve their bodies — their "temples" — for the afterlife. Connecting these dots, she reasoned that reincarnation was not only possible but perhaps inevitable.

Why such thoughts came to her now, she could not explain. She had always been contemplative, but this stream of reflection felt different, almost urgent. Still, she pushed it aside as she stepped off the bus in Ana Regina, her mind quickly shifting to more immediate concerns: planning the list of dishes she would prepare to sell at the construction site the next day.

THE LINE TO ROWENA'S FOOD stand grew longer by the minute. The first man who had bought a plate of cookup rice with curried chicken could not contain his delight; he walked the site announcing to coworkers that a lady was "up front sellin' some gud finga-lickin' food!" That news was manna to many of the bachelors on the construction crew — men without doting mothers or sisters to cook for them. The old saying that necessity is the best teacher was never lost on Rowena. Pushed by a need to provide for her children, recognizing a demand, and armed with the skill to meet it, she seized the day.

In short order, Rowena established a system to run her little enterprise. "Cash?" she would ask. If the answer was yes, she filled the order and collected payment—bills into the left pocket of her apron, coins into the right. If credit was requested, she produced an exercise book from the side of her basket, recorded name, address, order, and price in neat columns, then served the meal. By the third day, having memorized the workers' particular tastes, she rarely needed to look up until the line was gone. The quality of her food, the efficiency of her system, and her beauty drew even married men to her stand—teasing each other about "who isn't eating whose wife's food anymore"—and the amusement made her days fly by.

On the fourth day at the site, as on the previous three, Rowena was so absorbed in her routine that she almost failed to notice the last man in line—until he spoke.

"What is a beautiful woman like you doing on a construction site, selling food?"

Rowena looked up—and gasped. Her mouth went dry, her knees went weak, and her heart hammered so fiercely she wanted to fold her arms over her chest to calm it. But her arms did not obey. The man stood there, admiring her, his smile the most dazzling, gold-studded grin she had ever seen. She could not look away. He was two or three inches taller than her five-foot-five, solidly built, with a caramel complexion that seemed to catch the late-morning sun like tempered glass. He wore gray from Fedora to alligator-skin shoes, the ensemble put together with effortless class. His smile radiated from deep in his eyes — eyes that felt eerily familiar, as if she had known that gaze in another life. She shivered inwardly and re-examined herself. Since her betrothal and the sudden slide from newlywed to young widow, vanity had taken a back seat. She remembered the mirror above the second-hand vanity in the little rented room — how thin she had grown. *Pull yourself together,* she told herself.

She broke the spell, looked down at her baskets, and without waiting for him to ask, began listing the dishes, opening and closing lids as she spoke: "I have curried shrimp, curried pork, black-eyed peas cook-up rice, white rice, dhall —"

"And you cooked all of this? You alone?" he asked.

She listened for more than the question. He meant more than information. She looked up and said, simply, "Yes, I did."

18

Then she waited. Still smiling, he shook his Fedora-capped head and said, "Interesting woman!" He extended a hand. "Vernon Lane."

"Rowena …" She hesitated over which surname to use—Daniels or Alleyne—but smiled and offered a name that masked the awkwardness: "Everyone calls me 'Rowie'. Of course, here they call me 'The Lunch Lady,' as you probably already know." She took his hand.

What she felt the instant their palms touched was like electricity—though she had never been electrocuted in her life, the surge felt as if megawatts had shot through her. The energy yanked her into another dimension, another era. In a flash she glimpsed them as a young couple building a house—a castle—together. "Haddy," he called, and she answered, "Yes, Ebrima?"

"I think I'll try your curried shrimp with black-eyed peas cook-up and … what do you have today, mauby or sorrel?" Vernon asked.

Rowena's soul snapped back to the present. She broke eye contact and looked down at her baskets to steady herself. She had experienced reveries before—dreams and nightmares that sometimes felt like other lives—but never had she met anyone in them. This time felt different, and it felt like awakening. She had long read about reincarnation and other mysteries; now she was convinced something within her could connect across dimensions, a deeper layer of consciousness stirring to life. From his features she guessed Vernon was mixed Amerindian and Alkebulan — and somehow, he was part of this stirring.

She met his gaze again and, trusting the pull in her chest, served his order. *This is not just an accident,* she thought. Then, with the practiced smile of a woman who had learned to keep life moving, she handed him his plate.

FIVE

As Rowena had come to deduce from the many volumes of history, philosophy, religion, mysticism, and metaphysics she had devoured over the years, humans had grown so intellectual that little outside of rational explanation appealed to them. She herself was more open-minded. Over the three months since she first met Vernon, their relationship had developed naturally, seamlessly. Rowena felt as though they had been together from the moment she first became aware of her own existence — in this lifetime, at least — especially considering the vision she had.

When she shared her feelings, Vernon told her, "I feel the same way too, Row. I wonder if it has anything to do with our heritages."

He was Wai Wai and Malinke mixed, confirming her first impression. What fascinated her most about the Malinke part, as he related his family's story, was that his ancestors refused to live as enslaved people. They had escaped the plantation to which they were taken, carving out their own existence in freedom.

Rowena had also been right in thinking he was more than a foreman at the construction site. Vernon owned a construction company and had secured the subcontract for the hospital expansion. On the day they met — or reunited, as they would later call it — she had asked him, "Cash or credit?", certain he would say "cash." And he did. But after finishing his meal, sitting on a bench one of his workers had brought him, he looked at the tab she had given him and said:

"For the whole month."

Rowena furrowed her brow. "What do you mean?"

Vernon smiled. "I want to pay you in advance for the whole month."

"Now why would you want to do that?" she asked.

That smile again. "Because your food is very good — and with all these hungry fellows here, I'm afraid you might sell out my portion if I don't pay ahead."

After some protest and convincing, the matter was settled.

Later that day, at home, Rowena could hardly contain her excitement as she explained to her mother and sister what had transpired — leaving out the out-of-body experience, of course.

"God doesn't come, but He does send," she beamed. "Lord knows I've had my share of struggles since Joseph died. God just knows my heart."

Maudeline and Rosemarie exchanged a look, silently wondering if the "He" Rowena spoke of was God — or the mysterious man in question. Either way, it soon became clear that Rowena had begun to see Vernon as a savior, one for whom, as they later put it, "she lost all sense of rational thinking."

Five months into their relationship, one calm Sunday afternoon, they sat on the seawall together, the vast Atlantic seeming to beckon them toward the horizon.

"I strongly believe you belong in my mother's native village," Vernon said suddenly.

Rowena turned her head, brow furrowed. "Why?"

Vernon tossed a stone onto the beach, where the tide had receded, and without looking at her, replied, "It's just a feeling. Ever since we met, I've been thinking more about that village — and dreaming about it. And you always appear in the dreams, in one form or another. In one dream, we moved somewhere vaguely familiar, and just as I was about to remember it clearly, the dream ended."

Now he turned to face her.

Rowena held his gaze. "Uhm! You mean Ants Grove? Or Victoria?"

"No, no. Shoots! I never told you, did I?" He shook his head. "You already know I was born in Ants Grove and grew up in Victoria, but only my father was native to Ants Grove. My mother was born in a little village called Kumakha, on the East Bank of Demerara. It has a very unique and interesting history." He cocked his head, eyes narrowing in thought.

"What?" Rowena asked, her curiosity alive on her face.

"You love to read about pre-slavery Alkebulan," Vernon said, nodding. "Maybe that's why I believe you'd feel at home among my mother's people."

"And why do you believe I'd feel at home among them?" she asked, tilting her head.

"Well," Vernon replied, "other than the first seven months after they were brought from Alkebulan to British Guiana, they never lived enslaved."

Now Rowena tilted her head further. He had her full attention.

"According to the legend passed down to us," Vernon continued, "my great-great-great-great-great grandmother, a Malinke woman known as *Edna the Warrior Queen*, who was herself a great-great-great granddaughter of Abu-Bakr, grandson of Mari Djata, organized a group of other captured Alkebulans who longed for freedom. They escaped the plantation—and were never captured again. They named the place Kumakha. When you meet the elders of the village, they'll gladly regale you with tales of our ancestors. They take great pride in continuing the line of griots of the Ashanti people."

The ocean rolled gently, a wave sliding up the sand before retreating in slow motion. The sun mirrored the sea, its last rays slipping behind the horizon.

"We must go before it gets too dark," Rowena said, standing and brushing off her skirt. She cast a glance at the sea, then back at Vernon, who had risen too. "Interestingly," she said, taking his hand, "I've read quite a bit about the Mandé people of West Africa—of whom the Asantes are a subgroup, and the Ashanti a further subgroup."

Moving together as if one, they stepped off the seawall and began walking home in stride.

"I can't wait to meet your mother's people," Rowena said, her voice alight with anticipation.

SIX

After a day-long journey across the Essequibo and Demerara rivers, Rowena, Vernon, and their three-year-old daughter, Shiela, arrived in Georgetown around 3:30 p.m. on a Monday in late September of 1958. Rowena was as excited as she was nervous. She had traveled to the capital city before with her parents, and though she was accustomed to its hustle and bustle, she always told herself she could never live there. Each time she returned to the safety of her rural world, steeped in its bourgeois customs and traditions, she would exhale in relief, praying her next trip would be far off.

Now, seated on the horse-drawn cart Vernon had hired, her daughter already perched beside her and their belongings loaded behind, Rowena glanced back at the Ferry Stelling. Passengers rushed to and from, and she wondered how long it would be before she ever returned to the Essequibo Coast, which already felt like a world away.

Leaving was neither easy nor hard. The women on both sides of her family had objected to her departure with Vernon to a village no one had ever heard of. Her father's objection was different: Rowena had convinced her mother to keep the three boys until she became "properly situated" in her new life. Harold Daniels loved his daughter and adored his grandsons. He took pride in her independence and often gave her sound, practical advice. He spoiled the boys with gifts and stories from his own youth — especially his years as a porknocker in the hinterland, where he made his fortune before returning to Danielstown, the village his parents had founded by purchasing the plantation on which they had once labored until emancipation. There they had also established the first post office on the Essequibo Coast.

Harold had raised his family in relative comfort, later retiring as postmaster after selling the post office to the government. He was content in his twilight years. Day visits from his grandsons were one thing; raising them full-time was quite another. At his age, he wanted freedom from the burdens of parenting.

Rowena was still reflecting on these changes — the financial and social security her family's enterprise had brought them — when a large green roadside sign caught her eye: **"Welcome to Agricola Village."**

She cocked her head. *Agricola? Why does that name ring a bell?*

"Agricola," she murmured aloud. Shiela looked up, thinking her mother was speaking to her. Rowena patted her daughter's hand and glanced back at the sign as it shrank in the distance. Turning her head, she met Vernon's eyes and was startled to see him studying her.

"You okay?" he mouthed, half-smiling, half-concerned.

It amazed her how often he seemed to sense her inner struggles. She smiled to reassure him, though the name *Agricola* still echoed faintly in her mind.

FROM ITS GEOGRAPHY TO ITS people to its vibrant cultural life, Kumakha was unlike any village Rowena had ever known. Just as Vernon had promised, she felt instantly at home among his people.

When they arrived, her new cousins-in-law literally lifted her and Shiela off the cart, passing them from arm to arm, showering them with hugs, kisses, and warm greetings. Rowena felt dizzy once her feet touched the ground again and steadied herself on Vernon's arm.

"We hear so much bout yuh, we souzun-in-law!" exclaimed one older woman, whose features and presence suggested she was a mother.

"We suh happy fuh see yuh!" said another, around Rowena's own age, her skin dark as a moonless night and smooth as polished stone.

Rowena quickly noticed that nearly everyone — men and women alike — shared a similar complexion and texture, with subtle variations.

"Eh eh! Well look how pretty we lil couzun is!" another woman exclaimed, scooping up Shiela and pinching her cheek before turning to Vernon, who was unloading luggage with the help of two male cousins. "Muh couzun, yuh strike gold eah. Wheh yuh find dis beautiful woman from?"

One woman, however, hung back. "Ah hope yuh gon like de place an' stay," she said coolly, avoiding Rowena's gaze.

Rowena offered a polite smile. "Well, if I am to judge by the welcome I've received, I'll certainly stay. I like the place already — and most of all, I like all of you."

Almost with disdain, the aloof woman shot back, "Why yuh tauk like dat? Yuh tink yuh betta dan we?"

Gasps and *suck teeth* rippled through the group. "Is wuh do she, Leviah?" someone demanded.

The older woman who had greeted Rowena first stepped between them, brushing a bug from Rowena's hair. "Sheh gon stay, Leviah. Is none ah yuh business." Then she took Rowena gently by the arm, chatting cheerfully as she led her toward the house Vernon had rented. Her efforts at distraction did little to ease Rowena's bewilderment, and she almost glanced back at Leviah—until Vernon suddenly appeared, swept her into his arms, and said:

"Close your eyes and don't open them till I tell you."

He carried her across the threshold, explaining as he did: "According to Kumakha culture, this is the third most important matrimonial ritual. Since neither of us was raised here, we missed out on the first two. Welcome to your new home!" He kissed her lips and set her down. "You can open your eyes now."

Rowena did so and slowly turned in a full circle, taking in the living room and its fixtures. Every piece of furniture she had once dreamed of buying was there, placed exactly as she had imagined. The floor-to-ceiling China cabinet stood flush against the wall opposite the door. The floral-patterned three-piece couch, with a purpleheart coffee table at its center, rested atop a Persian rug arranged like a semicircle. At either side of the curtained windows were two lacquered rocking chairs. The walls were painted her favorite pale turquoise blue, the moldings violet.

Rowena smiled, recalling Vernon once teasing her that the combination smacked of "Van Gogh syndrome," an allusion to eccentricity. Meeting his gaze now, his smile sent a warm quiver through her. She longed to be in his arms again, but reminded herself there were still other rooms to explore.

"Put her down," she told Vernon, "So we can inspect our new home together."

Sheila dashed to her mother's side and clutched her hand. Together, the three of them moved from room to room: living room, dining room, kitchen, and two bedrooms. Finally, they stepped outside to examine the outhouse a few feet from the back door, still the norm in the village.

Rowena was overwhelmed. She had embarked on a new chapter of life, and all the signs — even the cryptic ones — seemed to point toward a great future.

SEVEN

Six months had flown by like the wink of an eye — or so it seemed to Rowena. To think of all they had accomplished in so short a time made her dizzy.

She straightened from the hoe she had been working with in the kitchen garden, stretched her body with a long exhale, then walked over to a wooden bench under the house and sat down.

"Are you tired, Mommy?" asked Sheila, who was playing nearby with two cousins her age.

"Mommy just wants to rest her feet a little, Sweetie," Rowena replied.

"Oh!" Sheila said, before returning to her game.

Rowena watched her daughter — a bundle of joy and peace in this new world — and thought of her sons back on the Essequibo Coast. Once a month, her mother wrote letters with updates on the boys, their grandfather's joy in having them close, and her own ceaseless worries: *Are you sleeping under a mosquito net? Do you wear long boots to protect yourself from snake bites? Is there running water in the village? Don't spend too much time in the hot sun tending that garden...*

Rowena had to be careful not to reveal too much about life in Kumakha, lest her mother become needlessly agitated. Neither her mother nor her sister could ever have adjusted to this simpler, freer existence — so unlike the bourgeois life with its heavy cloak of social pretenses.

Though she and Vernon were building their own house mostly by themselves on the lot leased from Aunt Drusilla, the progress felt deeply gratifying. Together, they were creating a stable foundation for their children. Rowena felt a sense of security she had never known before.

Yes, she had grown up financially secure, cushioned by the comforts of her social class. But as a beautiful young woman from a well-to-do family, her fate had never been her own. It had been in her parents' hands — or, more precisely, her father's. When he had married her off to Joseph Alleyne, he had effectively washed his hands of her. Throughout that marriage she had felt like an orphaned child, abandoned, and forgotten.

Now, hearing how happy her father was to have the boys with him, she could not help but silently thank Vernon. He had unlocked the intrepid adventurer within her — the one she had long hidden, inspired by the great women she had read about, praying for a miracle to free her from the invisible prison built by patriarchy.

And here I am, she thought, *with a man who gives me the freedom to live as I choose.*

She recalled the playful exchange they'd had on the ferry at Adventure Stelling.

"How come you didn't break any bones when you fell out of Heaven, Vern?" she had teased.

He had chuckled, holding back laughter. "Because I landed in the softest bosom on Earth."

She had smacked his arm playfully, smiling.

Now, freed from the heavy dawn clouds that had drenched the earth in rain, the sun warmed the air, pulling dampness up like steam. The forest responded with a living symphony: birds trilled, insects droned, and hidden creatures sang unseen. Flowers and trees released their fragrances, caressing Rowena's senses. She closed her eyes and tipped her head back, savoring the moment.

Then, without warning, an image flashed before her inner vision — blurred at first, then sharpening.

Leviah. She appeared, dressed as an *Iyanifa* priestess, clad in a flowing white gown that reached the ground, holding an *Oshe Shango* staff.

Rowena's chest tightened. She tried to rise, but her body would not move. She tried to open her eyes, but they remained sealed. She tried to call for Vernon, but no sound escaped her lips.

Leviah stood before her, eyes locked, lifting the staff high above her head, chanting in a language Rowena did not know — Ebo, though she did not realize it. The chant grew stronger, vibrating through the air.

Panic surged in Rowena's mind. *Sheila!* She willed herself to turn her head toward where her daughter played, but her body remained frozen.

The chanting rose, the staff gleaming as Leviah held it aloft.

Then came a burst of thunder. Lightning split the sky.

EIGHT

After striking gold — literally — in his mine up the Potaro River, Bael Walter Byrne Jr. bought land in Victoria Village (VV) and built a house. The villagers soon nicknamed it *The Byrne Mansion* for its size, unique architecture, and elegance. It was modeled after a photograph of an Irish baron's mansion his father had once framed and hung on their living room wall in Ants Grove. As a boy, Bael Jr. had been fascinated by the image, even though the house itself had no connection to his bloodline. His father, Bael Sr., had found the photograph tucked inside a discarded valise during his teenage years of service to the Irish baron. To him, owning the picture was the closest he thought he would ever come to such grandeur. But his son, with grit and fortune, proved that dreams could be made real.

Though the Byrnes had lived comfortably in Ants Grove, their move to VV was a significant rise up the socioeconomic ladder.

Victoria Village, the first officially established freeholding village of emancipated Alkebulans in British Guiana, was a cultural mecca — a crossroads where centuries-old Alkebulan traditions, preserved through slavery, mingled with modern values. Unlike Georgetown, the capital with its bustling mercantile and cosmopolitan character dominated by the non-Alkebulan merchant class, Victoria Village attracted the emerging Alkebulan and Dougla bourgeoisie. These groups — proud of their heritage and intent on cementing identity — sought to immerse themselves in cultural continuity.

Belonging to both worlds, Bael Jr. and his wife, Cecelia, were determined to lift their children, Vernon and Florence, into a higher stratum. Public school, they believed, no longer suited them. Florence was sent to a Catholic convent in Georgetown; Vernon, to a Dutch boarding school in New Amsterdam, Berbice.

The transition was difficult at first, but Vernon eventually fell into rhythm and thrived. His success pleased Bael Jr., a man of few words, deliberate in action, and focused intently on family and business.

Shaped by the culture of British Guiana's plantocracy, Bael Jr. carried the privilege of mixed Irish and Amerindian descent — a status that granted easier access to resources and social mobility. Yet he never flaunted this advantage. Humble by nature, he divided his life between his family and his beloved mine. A homebody when in VV, he rarely socialized, never drank, and often repeated: *"People can't be trusted anymore, not even your own kin."* He warned Vernon: *"Wealth makes you a target for envy, and good looks make you a target for jealousy. We of mixed ethnicity are either blessed or cursed with both, depending on the circumstance. That is one of our great dilemmas."*

BAEL WALTER BYRNE SR. had been born and raised in Ireland until his mid-teens. Family lore painted him as a "troublemaker," though no one knew the details. Whatever his offense, it was serious enough to land him on a ship bound for British Guiana with other Irishmen, indentured rather than imprisoned.

After completing his contract on a sugar plantation in West Demerara, Byrne Sr. packed his meager possessions into a duffel bag and headed into the hinterland, where he found work at a gold mine owned by another Irishman. Handsome, silver-tongued, and hardworking, he soon caught the eye of the eldest daughter of a nearby Amerindian chief.

Within a year, they were married and expecting their first child. She was renowned not only for her beauty and loyalty to family but also for her skill with bow and arrow. Yet tragedy soon shattered their union.

Eight months after the birth of their third child — and only son—his wife and their second daughter perished when their canoe was caught in a *turn tide*, a deadly whirlpool. Their bodies were discovered three days later, floating downriver.

The eldest daughter, still barely more than a child herself, assumed the dual roles of sister and surrogate mother.

Heartbroken, Byrne Sr. left the mine and resettled with his children in Ants Grove, on the East Coast of Demerara. He never remarried. Yet he never entirely severed ties to the mine, carrying both grief and memory with him until the end of his days.

Two weeks later, after securing the concession under Buckman Tony's steady supervision, Bael Walter Byrne Jr. accompanied Joseph on the long trip downriver and across the Demerara. The journey was grueling yet oddly refreshing, a steady alternation of paddling, walking, and waiting for ferries. To Joseph it was routine; to Bael, it was a new frontier.

When they finally approached the East Bank, Joseph's mood seemed to change. He stood straighter in the bow of the boat; his gaze fixed on the tree line ahead. "We close now," he said quietly, almost reverently. "This is where my people settled — where we still live free."

Bael felt something stir in his chest. He could not explain it, but there was a weight in the air, a kind of ancestral energy that seemed to hum through the ground and the river alike.

They came ashore where a narrow track curved into dense greenery. Joseph led the way, his steps quick but measured, as though each footfall respected sacred earth. Within the hour, the path opened into a village unlike any Bael had seen.

The houses were modest, framed in timber and palm, but neat, their yards swept smooth as if every morning began with ritual. A central clearing, shaded by an immense Kumakha tree, spread wide before them. Around it, villagers bustled — children chasing chickens, women grinding cassava, men repairing nets and tools.

41

Yet when Joseph stepped into the clearing, all motion seemed to pause.

"Joseph home!" someone called, and a ripple of greetings followed. Then eyes turned toward Bael. A stranger. Tall, broad-shouldered, skin burnished by mine work, dressed in city trousers and shirt. His mixed heritage was evident, but his bearing spoke of discipline.

Joseph raised his voice: "This is Bael Byrne—my brother of labor, my friend, my partner. He come see we way."

At once, an elder stepped forward. His hair was silver, his back bent but steady, his eyes still sharp as river stones. He studied Bael in silence, then nodded slowly. "Welcome. All who come here must honor those who walked before. You will sit, you will listen, and you will learn."

Bael inclined his head, humbled.

That evening, as drums began to echo through the clearing and the fire blazed high, Joseph leaned close to him. "Tonight, you will hear the story of Edna."

The name struck him like a bell. "Edna?"

"Yes," Joseph said, eyes gleaming. "Edna the Warrior Queen. Our ancestress. She was the one who led the first to escape. She was Ashanti, descendant of griots and princes. They say the blood of her courage still runs in all of us."

As the fire cracked and the drummers shifted into a steady rhythm, the elder stood and lifted his arms. His voice rolled like thunder, weaving history into song.

"She was taken from Kumasi… chained, but never broken. She came across the water, but the water could not hold her spirit. She walked the plantation earth — but earth could not bind her feet. And so, she gathered the strong, the willing, the fierce… and they fled, never to be slaves again. Here, under this Kumakha tree, they built freedom."

Bael listened, the hair rising on his arms. Though the tale belonged to Joseph's bloodline, he felt it pulling at him, too — as if the legend itself reached out across time and ethnicity, demanding recognition.

The elder's chant swelled: *"We are the children of Edna. We are the freeborn of Kumakha. Her fire is our fire. Her blood is our blood."*

Bael's eyes met Joseph's. For a fleeting instant, he thought he saw the same golden shimmer in Joseph's gaze that he had once glimpsed in O'Hare's — the unmistakable mark of destiny.

And though he could not know it then, Bael Walter Byrne Jr., by stepping into Kumakha that night, had bound his own lineage forever to Edna's.

NINE

Back at the mine, the clang of pickaxes and the groan of timber braces sounded different to Bael Walter Byrne Jr. than they had before. Gold still shimmered under his watch, and wealth still accumulated under his name, but he could no longer shake the awareness that his fortune, his labor, and even his very breath was woven into a story far older and far larger than his own. What he had seen and felt in Kumakha had changed him.

Growing up in Ants Grove and frequenting Victoria Village, he had always been familiar with Alkebulan culture. Yet what he experienced in Kumakha left him in utter awe. The Kumakhans were unique in every sense of the word—from their complexion (and he had seen very dark Alkebulans) down to their aura and even their speech. Now he could finally put Joseph's personality and character into perspective, connecting him to a reality that had previously seemed unfathomable. For the first time, he understood where this "different negro," as others had ignorantly labeled him, might have come from.

On his second day in the village, Bael sat under the great kumakha tree beside Joseph and the rest of his family. The chair beneath him, carved from a single tree trunk and varnished to such a sheen that he could see his own reflection in it, seemed like more than just a seat—it was a throne of memory, one that linked him to generations he had not yet met. In his hand, a polished ceramic cup of maubee; beside him, Joseph, sipping from an identical one.

Joseph's family numbered seven in all—three sisters and four brothers, of whom he was the eldest. He had gone to the mine as a rite of passage, and his kin held their pride in him like a banner. Like Bael, he had refused to splurge or gamble away his earnings. The two young men shared a rare bond of respect, their lives braided together by trust and discipline. But amid all the familial warmth, Bael found his gaze drawn to one in particular.

Margerie Lane. The first daughter, third-born among her siblings. Her reddish headwrap framed a face both soft and commanding, while her plain green cotton blouse with its white frills, paired with a long skirt sweeping her ankles, somehow made her appear regal. A cascade of wooden and beaded necklaces rested against her chest, descending in size from small to large, marking her presence with quiet authority. Barefoot, she glided across the packed earth, each step so effortless she seemed less to walk than to float.

Bael could not take his eyes off her. He was captivated by her skin, densely dark and flawlessly smooth, but even more by the aura of majesty she carried with ease.

When the family laid out the food — a feast spread across a massive communal table — Bael joined them, watching as Mr. Lane blessed the meal and poured libation. That meal, fragrant with cassava bread, pepper pot, and wild fruits, was unlike any he had ever tasted. And it etched itself into his memory forever.

The elders took the timing of his visit as a sign: it had coincided with the full moon. To the Kumakhans, such alignment meant an omen. Whatever path Bael was destined to walk, it would now be brightened. No hidden obstacle would cause him to stumble, for the ancestors themselves, with Ngewo the Supreme Creator, would guide his steps.

After the food and games and hours of laughter, when the compound finally grew quiet, Joseph asked his sister to keep their guest company while he stayed outside to absorb the village's nocturnal spirit.

So it was that Bael Walter Byrne Jr. found himself lying in a hammock under the calabash tree, parallel to another where Margerie sat cross-legged, her silhouette radiant beneath the moonlight. The night sang with insects and river wind, and Margerie's voice — gentle, melodic, angelic — wove itself through the dark.

Bael closed his eyes and felt the moment strike deeper than mere attraction. This was recognition. Something older than time itself stirred in him, whispering that he had not stumbled into her life by chance. He had found his soulmate.

Six months later, in full Kumakhan style and tradition, Bael and Margerie were married.

TEN

And here I am, eighteen years later—Vernon Bael Byrne, the only son of Bael Walter Jr. and Margerie Lou Byrne—carrying on the tradition, spending my eighteenth birthday among my maternal folk as a rite of passage. It was also the first holiday from boarding school that I was spending in Kumakha. The previous ones I had spent with classmates, either at our home in Victoria Village or at theirs in different parts of the country.

Much about Kumakha had changed since the days when my mother used to bring my sister and me as children. Even my grandparents' house, where my mother had grown up and where my father had stayed on his first visit, looked different. Uncle Joseph and one of his brothers, Uncle Oscar—both of whom had also worked in the mine—had rebuilt it. In fact, they had rebuilt the entire Byrne compound into one of the most impressive in the village. Grandpa Lane and Grandma Ursilla were the only ones living there now, and they were elated to have me around, determined to spoil me at every chance they got.

Grandpa, in his early eighties, was still robust, his muscles and veins bulging beneath his midnight-dark skin, his mind sharp as razor grass, as the locals would say. No longer working his plot of coffee to sustain the family, he now spent his time carving wooden sculptures, a passion he had cherished since childhood. His voice thundered whenever he spoke, yet it carried no trace of anger. The glow of kindness and compassion in his eyes softened its impact, making his presence a joy.

Grandma, however, seemed to defy all laws of nature and biology. In her late seventies, she could easily have passed for a woman in her forties, often confusing strangers as to whether she was the mother of her daughters or their sibling. Beauty, strength, agility, grace, wisdom, and humility were all perfectly woven into her feminine frame—her flawless dark-chocolate complexion and sensuous proportions adding to the aura she carried.

The house itself was two stories, with most of the bedrooms upstairs—the first to the left of the staircase being my mother's. My uncles had restored all the rooms exactly as their original occupants had kept them while growing up, so they were always ready for family visits. This time, my mother and father occupied hers. My

sister, Florence, stayed in one of my aunts'
rooms, while I took Uncle Joseph's.

The morning after our arrival, I woke before the
others, pulled on a pair of short pants and a
white "wifebeater," and went downstairs.
Grandpa, dressed in his usual dark-brown
jumper with no shirt underneath, his white
mane of hair neatly slicked back, was already
sitting at the dining table. It was laden with an
array of sumptuous dishes fit for a royal
breakfast, and he sat reading a newspaper with
the calm authority of a patriarch. Grandma was
still in the kitchen, stirring something on the
stove.

When she heard my footsteps on the stairs, she
turned and cheered, "Good morning, my
grandson! I hope you had a pleasant night's
rest." The aroma of the food matched the love in
her voice.

"Good morning," Grandpa thundered in his
deep, resonant tone.

"Good morning, Grandma and Grandpa!" I
replied, going first to the kitchen to give her a
hug and a kiss on the cheek. Then into the dining
room, I hugged Grandpa and kissed his

forehead before slipping into the bathroom to wash my face and brush my teeth.

"Don't take a year and a day in there now and let this food get cold," Grandma called out—a typical Guianese saying, meaning hurry up and come eat your heart out! And that I surely did, once everyone had gathered at the table.

Word of my being in the village to celebrate my eighteenth birthday spread quickly. A steady stream of cousins flowed in and out of my grandparents' house throughout that first day, which was a Thursday. Those who didn't bring gifts came with the hope of receiving some. Toward evening, my favorite female cousin, Angella, arrived with the costume I would wear during the *kumfaah* ceremony, scheduled for the next evening, marking my rite of passage into the Kumakhan pantheon of ordained princes.

My father had already told me about the pomp and splendor of his own rite of passage, how his maternal clan had spared no expense to make it one of the most extravagant experiences of his life—second only to his wedding ceremony with my mother. Handing me the outfit, Angella said, "Go put it on and come let me see how you look. It's hard to imagine you in this type of clothes because you stand out among us like a sole kidney bean in a pale of black beans."

I laughed so hard I nearly gave myself stomach cramps. "How do you come up with these things?" I asked.

Angella gave me a stern stare. "I'm glad I can make you laugh. Now go put on the clothes," she said again, settling herself into a chair in the lounge that all the upstairs bedrooms shared.

I hadn't even known that black beans existed, but her analogy intrigued me, and I wanted to know what subliminal meaning she was hinting at. The obvious point was clear — my sister, Florence, and I were the ones in that bloodline mixed with other ethnicities, Amerindian and Irish in our case. But Angella, unlike most of the older relatives who guarded tradition, had always been willing to share. She would sit for hours and tell me everything she knew, even the parts others preferred to relegate to oblivion.

I had read somewhere that griots always knew who among the next generation was called to receive and carry forward the cultural memory. Five years my senior, Angella — with all the gifts of a griot — may have singled me out because of my curiosity, the questions I asked, and the attentiveness with which I listened. Or perhaps it was simply the natural order of things — the genetic selection of memory and voice at work through time.

I HAD ATTENDED KUMFAAH CEREMONIES in Victoria Village before, but ours in Kumakha was otherworldly — an event that seemed to take place in another realm, in another age, and I was merely dreaming it. The costumes were fashioned from leaves, feathers, and animal hides, intricately woven into patterns evoking images of the great Alkebulan deities.

At the center of the compound, the bonfire glowed within a perfect twenty-foot circle, its flames neither flaring wildly nor dimming out, but steady and alive, like a breathing spirit. The sweet aroma that rose from it caressed my senses, sending a soothing calm through my body. Then came the drums. The rhythm, "talking" beneath the palms and fingers of the players, reverberated through time and space with a melody I had never heard before. It enveloped my soul, pulling me into a trance.

Twelve of us — six males and six females — danced around the fire, chanting the song they had taught us the day before. I could not recall the words, yet my lips moved in perfect rhythm with the chant. After four or five laps, the aroma, the rhythm, the melody, and the circular motion conspired together and sent me spiraling into a vortex. Before I could react, I was shot into another dimension, dark and warm.

I cannot say whether it felt like the blink of an eye or an eternity, but I awoke to soft hands caressing my shoulders. Following Kumakhan tradition, I was required to spend the rest of that night — and the entire following day and night — in a benab prepared for the culmination of the rite of passage. During that time, the deities, working with the ancestors, would guide my soulmate, a virgin of the highest order, to me as a reward for successfully entering manhood. After the consecration of our union, the clan would plan our wedding.

But I had also heard the whispers: the deities did not discriminate in matters of the heart. Sometimes, the oracle's choice fell upon a cousin, a niece or nephew — even a sibling. Among royals across the world, such unions were not only tolerated but expected. In Kumakha, however, such outcomes carried both blessing and dilemma.

I turned onto my back and looked up. Into familiar eyes. A face framed by thick, cascading braids glowed in the soft light of a candle set in the corner of the benab. My heart nearly stopped.

"Leviah," I whispered. "Why are you in here?"

We were on a mattress made of crocus bags stuffed with dry grass, covered by a quilt so finely crafted it seemed more art than bedding, placed on a clay floor daubed to perfection. My mind wrestled with what I had heard about the oracles of matrimony. Did the elders know it was her? Or had she forced her way in?

Her eyes never left mine. They were tender, luminous, brimming with a love that pervaded the close space between us. Other than glimpses of her as a little girl when my mother brought me here, I had not seen her again until the night before. During the opening of the ceremony, when the dancers sat in a circle, she had been directly opposite me. Unlike the other girls, who looked away whenever our eyes met, Leviah held my gaze, unflinching. I had thought little of it then. Angella's teasing words about how I stood out among them lingered too heavily in my mind. But now, she had all my attention.

56

As I sat there, waging a moral war within my soul, I realized the truth of my father's saying: knowledge is both a blessing and a curse. All my female cousins on my mother's side were beautiful—unquestionably so. But Leviah … Leviah was something more. A goddess, radiant in a class all her own.

Perhaps sensing my turmoil, she took my right hand and clasped it between her palms.

"Don't worry, my cousin," she whispered, her voice as enchanting as her beauty. "No one knows I'm here. They're all drunk or too tired to stir before daybreak. But I'll be long gone before then."

ELEVEN

Her words lingered in the air like smoke from the bonfire outside, thick with meaning, impossible to disperse. My pulse thundered in my ears as I studied her face—so familiar, yet newly revealed.

"Levitia," I said again, her name catching in my throat. "If they find you here..."

"They won't." She leaned closer, the candlelight dancing across her smooth, obsidian skin. "You don't understand, do you? I felt it from the fire, from the drums. The ancestors called me. Not anyone else. Me."

Her conviction struck me harder than any blow. Tradition warned of boundaries, yet here she was, speaking as though boundaries meant nothing in the presence of spirit. I wanted to protest, to remind her of the whispers that oracles could bind cousin to cousin. But the words dissolved before reaching my lips.

I thought of my father, Bael Walter Jr., who had once told me that destiny seldom announces itself politely; it breaks through in moments of confusion, dressed in the garments of taboo. Was this what he meant?

The rational part of me recoiled. I had seen enough of human frailty to know that desire can blind a man. Yet something deeper stirred—a current older than reason, older than memory, surging through me as though it belonged not to Vernon Bael Byrne, but to all the Byrne men and women before me, back to Edna herself.

Her eyes glowed like twin lanterns, steady, unafraid. She pressed my hand tighter. "You feel it too, don't you? The pull."

I swallowed hard. "I feel... something."

"No," she said firmly, her voice low but unwavering. "Not something. You feel *them*. The ancestors. The gods. Edna."

Her name—spoken here, now—sent a chill across my skin. I had not told her that I had dreamed of the Ashanti princess since boyhood, glimpses of a warrior woman in the shadows of my sleep, whispering to me across time. Yet Leviah's utterance made me certain: she knew.

Desire clawed at me. Taboo stood like a sentinel between us. And destiny... destiny wove the two together in a knot I could neither untangle nor ignore.

I closed my eyes, fighting for breath. I saw Edna in chains, refusing to bow. I saw Joao, Nkechi, the Kumakha tree, the laughter and the blood. I saw my own hands, not mine, but another's — striking fire from stone, weaving baskets, wielding a cutlass in defense of the clan.

When I opened my eyes, Levitia was still there, silent now, waiting. In her presence, I realized the truth: the bloodline of Edna was not meant to follow the rules of man. It bent them. Broke them. Reforged them in ways that frightened even those who believed themselves strong.

My hand, still clasped in hers, trembled — not from fear of her, but from the knowledge that in this benab, under the watch of spirits and ancestors, I was standing on the threshold of a fate I could not escape.

And somewhere deep within, a voice whispered: *This is how the line endures. Through fire. Through taboo. Through the choosing of souls, not the sanction of men.*

LEVIAH DID NOT RELEASE MY HAND. Instead, she drew it gently to her chest, pressing it over her heart. The steady rhythm of her pulse echoed through my palm, matching the drumming I had heard hours earlier. It was as if the bonfire outside had followed us into this benab, its rhythm living now in her body, in mine.

"You see?" she whispered. "It is already decided."

I wanted to resist, wanted to invoke the rules, the traditions, the whispered warnings of elders, but my voice was lost. Something larger was at work. I felt it, deep and undeniable.

The candle flame flickered. The air thickened. A sudden hush fell across the benab, as though even the insects had ceased their nighttime chorus. Then came a sound, low at first, then rising, a whispering chorus that seemed to circle the thatched walls. Words I could not understand, yet which filled me with recognition, as though the marrow of my bones knew their meaning.

Leviah closed her eyes and began to chant softly, a language older than Kumakha itself. The sound rose and fell like waves against the shore.

My skin prickled. My breath caught. For an instant, I saw her face change. Her features overlapped with those of another. A warrior queen with eyes like burning coals.

The hut swayed. My heart hammered. I tried to pull back, but her grip held me steady. "Don't be afraid," she murmured. "They are here. She is here."

And then I felt it. Not desire, not taboo. Something else, something deeper. A presence pressing down on me, surrounding me, entering me. My mind filled with images: a matronly figure under a Kumakha tree, dagger raised; the ambush of headhunters; the laughter of a people rediscovering freedom after generations of bondage. I felt their triumphs, their grief, their unyielding will.

When I opened my eyes, Leviah's face hovered inches from mine. She was smiling through tears. "They chose us," she said simply.

The flame leapt, flaring high, then steadied again. The whispering voices faded into silence, leaving behind a stillness so complete it rang louder than sound. In that silence, our lips met.

The kiss was no ordinary joining. It was fire and water, thunder and stillness, past and present colliding. The ancestors bore witness; the gods sealed the bond. The taboo dissolved like morning mist, leaving only the truth: we were not bound by man's rules, but by the covenant of spirit.

I pulled back, breathless, staring into her eyes. "This changes everything," I whispered.

"No," she corrected me gently. "It only reveals what was always written."

Outside, the first streak of dawn cut through the canopy, spilling pale gold into the benab. The light touched us both, as if blessing what had taken place.

And deep within me, a voice not my own resounded with certainty: *Through you, through her, Edna's bloodline continues. Through you, her legacy lives.*

TWELVE

Giving it everything she had, drawing on every faculty of her being, Rowena pulled and pulled until she finally yanked herself out of the sleep paralysis. She sprang to her feet and dashed toward Sheila, startling her and her cousin. Torso bent forward, she swept both little girls into her trembling but powerful arms, clutching them tightly against her body.

Sheila tried to look up at her mother but could not free her neck from the bear hug. She opened her mouth to speak, but Rowena cut her off.

"Shhhhh! Let's go inside. C'mon!"

Rowena glanced left and right, then guided the children quickly through the open back door, closing it firmly behind them. She hurried to the front and made sure the door was locked.

"What is wrong, Mommy?" Sheila asked, standing in the doorway between the kitchen and the dining room. Julie hovered obliquely behind her, just as confused as her cousin.

Rowena, unsure of what to say, looked at her daughter but saw them both. She had always made a habit of speaking to children as though they were adults, but this time she knew she had to choose her words carefully.

"Some things are difficult to explain, Sweetheart," she said at last. "To others who have not experienced them personally, they may not make sense."

Sheila frowned, then said softly, "Oh!" She turned to Julie, now at her side, the two girls looking to Rowena like life-size portraits framed against the doorway wall. The comparison struck her as strange. Why would her mind drift to painting now? Yet she was not oblivious to fine arts. One of the extravagances her father had invested in after selling the post office was a collection of post-emancipation paintings by artists newly free to document either their own lives or those of others during slavery's darkest days. The colonizers, though barred from profiting off slavery itself, had swiftly monopolized the artefacts of that defunct system. All things slavery-related had suddenly become fashionable, even "sexy."

"Tic toc! Tic toc! Tic toc!" The grandfather clock on the eastern wall of the dining room jolted

Rowena back. She looked up: 10:47. "Well, it's time to start cooking lunch," she announced to no one in particular, then stepped into the kitchen. Pausing in the doorway, she looked back. "Please, Sweethearts, play in the dining room where I can see you at all times."

"Ok, Mommy," Sheila said. "Ok, Auntie Rowie," Julie echoed.

Rowena smiled at them both. "Thank you, Babies." As she moved around the kitchen, she tried not to dwell on what had just happened. But the effort was futile. She had not experienced sleep paralysis since she was eight years old. And Leviah? She had only seen her twice since her arrival, and though she had felt strange vibes from her, she hadn't thought much of it until now.

Anyway, she told herself, *I have to get her off my mind.* But the thought clung like a weight. It felt less like dismissing a memory than waging another battle.

She began humming to distract herself as she reached into the cupboard for a pot. When the aluminum pots clattered together, their sound stirred a memory — the "invoking" she had attended just two weeks earlier. On the darkest nights of the year, priests and priestesses called the spirits of the ancestors through drums and chants. She had heard people say the drumming could "wake the dead," but she had wanted to see it for herself.

That night, she had gone with three of her sisters-in-law. They stood on the road in front of Mr. Smallie's yard, where the ceremony would take place. The turnout was larger than she had expected. Families she had never seen before filled the roadside; children ran about playing, unbothered by the nature of the ritual.

The priests and priestesses, dressed all in white, gathered in the yard. A ring of drummers encircled them, testing and tuning their instruments. Some leaned toward one another, talking quietly.

Mr. Smallie, the head priest, raised his torch in one hand and a shoulder-length staff in the other. He was tall and slender, with a narrow face, a pointed goatee, and eyes that danced whenever he spoke, and his voice was high-pitched and animated.

"Good night! Good night!" he cried, capturing the crowd. "Tonight, we come together to call on the ancestors — chief among them The Warrior

Queen of Kumakha — to commune with us, to bless us with health, freedom, prosperity, long life, or whatever omens they choose to reveal. So let us pour libation to those who have crossed into the other realm." He tipped his goblet and called out: "Cecelia Small! Moses Daniels! ..."

A faint humming began, melodic, solemn, growing into chanting. "Amazing grace, how sweet the sound that saved a wretch like me..." The drummers joined in, first lightly, playfully.

Rowena, almost against her will, began to sing. Her head swayed with the rhythm. The tempo quickened, and the drummers drew sounds from their skins unlike anything she had ever experienced. She felt her soul pulsing, as if rising toward her pores, pressing to break free.

She resisted, pulling herself back. Turning to her cousin-in-law, she whispered, "Jasmine, I can't take this drumming anymore. It's getting to my head. I want to go home."

Jasmine studied her. "Ok, wait fuh meh hey," she said, then slipped through the crowd, crossed into the yard, and whispered something to one of the priestesses.

The priestess turned her head, locking eyes with Rowena. It was Leviah. She smiled faintly, then turned back.

"And now today," Rowena muttered under her breath as she stirred rice on the stove. "Why me? Why has she been hostile to me since the day I got here?"

Maybe I should tell Vernon when he gets home. She paused. *Then again… maybe it's all coincidence.*

With effort, she pushed the thoughts aside and focused on more ordinary tasks. She finished cooking, served the food, and ate with the girls in silence, acutely aware that they were living in the most politically volatile period since emancipation in British Guiana.

The 1950s was a decade of political turmoil in British Guiana. On the one hand, the struggle for independence from Great Britain dominated the national discourse and, for a time, served as the glue — though gradually weakening — that held the various ethnic groups together as a nation. Breaking free from the yoke of colonialism was the one goal that everyone could agree upon. United, the people wielded greater power; fractured, they risked becoming pawns of the very empire they were trying to escape. Thus, ethnic harmony, or at least a semblance of it, was treated as an imperative force in the fight for independence.

Freedom from the oppressor transcended the rivalries that colonialism itself had fostered. Divide and rule. That had always been the strategy. *What a mess they left behind,* Rowena thought, recalling the bitter aftermath of the 1957 general elections. *None of it makes sense. Why do we need four different political parties, all claiming to fight for the same independence? How can we expect the British to take us seriously, to see us as worthy of autonomy, if we cannot even unite as one people, capable of self-government?*

The split of the People's Progressive Party (PPP) into two factions: one led by Cheddi Jagan, the other by Forbes Burnham, had laid bare the simmering division between the colony's two largest groups: East Indians and Alkebulans. That division had been brewing since the late 1800s, when East Indians were brought to British Guiana as indentured laborers to replace enslaved Africans who had gained their freedom. From the outset, the transition was marked by injustice. Many freed Africans had acquired land and sought to build independent livelihoods, but they were systematically denied access to credit and capital by colonial banks. Meanwhile, East Indian laborers, arriving with nothing but the clothes on their backs, were offered structured contracts, housing on plantations, and in some cases greater access to land and small loans.

This calculated economic imbalance created fertile ground for resentment. The Alkebulan community, locked out of opportunities to expand their holdings, saw their gains stunted, while the new arrivals were granted entry into the "free market." By the 1950s, the legacy of this divide, fanned by colonial administrators who played one group against the other, had erupted into ethnic clashes and riots, threatening to tear the colony apart just as the call for independence grew loudest.

As she worried about her parents and sister back on the Essequibo Coast, Rowena also felt grateful for Kumakha's isolation. Etched into the forest, three and a half miles east of the East Bank Demerara Public Road, the village seemed sheltered from the chaos sweeping across the country. Its population was overwhelmingly Alkebulan, with only a handful of mixed families, including one East Indian-Alkebulan, the other Chinese-Alkebulan. In Kumakha,

Rowena did not have to navigate the daily tension of divided streets and polarized loyalties.

There were, of course, other concerns, some spiritual, some personal, but nothing she could not meet with calm resolve and the fortitude of her faith. And as the years passed, she became deeply attuned to Kumakha's rhythms, its customs, culture, and traditions, until the village was no longer a place she had joined, but one she belonged to.

THIRTEEN

During the 1970s, when Michael Jacob Byrne came of age, Alkebulan consciousness and the drive to reconnect with the Motherland reached an all-time high in Guyana. With slavery long abolished, indentureship dissolved, and colonialism crumbling to its knees, the once-colonized seized the moment to reclaim their ancestral heritage. Trade unionism and grassroots activism had set the stage, and now an irrevocable cultural revolution was in motion.

The newly independent Cooperative Republic of Guyana, under the leadership of a president who himself was a descendant of enslaved Alkebulans, forged bold cultural and diplomatic ties with progressive leaders across Alkebula and India. From Ghana to Tanzania, from India to the Caribbean, Guyana positioned itself as part of a global movement of liberation. Reggae music added fuel to the fire. Bursting out of Jamaica and spreading like wildfire across the Caribbean and beyond, it became a drumbeat of resistance and pride, calling the youth to embrace their identity, wherever their roots lay.

Even the education system reflected this seismic shift. The colonial-era curriculum — stuffed with tales of European conquest and empire — was dismantled piece by piece. In its place came locally authored texts, written from the perspective of the formerly colonized, celebrating Alkebulan heroes, Indian martyrs, Caribbean thinkers, and indigenous traditions. For the first time, Guyanese children were being taught not only to know themselves but to see themselves at the center of history.

Growing up in Kumakha, a village steeped in unique cultural traditions and fortified by ancestral pride, Michael Byrne was nurtured by these currents of awakening. From birth, his mother and paternal grandparents fed him the stories of his forebears — their struggles, their victories, their spiritual powers. By eighteen, he had devoured every book in his mother's library, moved on to the shelves of the National Library in Georgetown, and became a familiar face at the Kumakha Local Library.

Though Creolese was the dialect of his everyday world, Michael spoke English with an impeccable British lilt, a legacy of colonial schooling layered with his own meticulous study. His hunger for knowledge stretched beyond the ordinary. His grasp of history and philosophy, and his restless curiosity about existence itself, set him apart. Those who met him sensed he was not just precocious, but marked — as if carrying wisdom from another realm.

That suspicion, in fact, had first arisen the moment he was born. The midwife who delivered him had seen hundreds of babies take their first breath, but never one like Michael. When she slapped his tiny buttocks, expecting the familiar wail, he did not cry. Instead, he made a sound, low, resonant, and strange, which chilled her to the spine.

Rowena, exhausted yet radiant, recognized it instantly. Her heart leapt with an intuition that needed no explanation. "Give him to me!" she commanded, reaching out with trembling arms. She pressed the infant to her bosom, whispering, "Shhh... I know you."

The midwife, bewildered and unnerved, fled the room without even looking back.

Michael's arrival had been no ordinary birth. From that first utterance, it was as though the ancestors themselves had announced: *the legacy will live on.*

Michael's teenage years unfolded against the backdrop of a surging tide of identity. Reggae blasted from every corner shop and beer garden, its heavy basslines rolling through the cane fields, carried by coastal breeze like the very heartbeat of the Caribbean. Bob Marley, Burning Spear, Peter Tosh — these were not just entertainers, but prophets. Their songs of liberation, of Jah, of Alkebulan, struck Michael like scripture.

When he walked through the village square in Kumakha, dreadlocked elders and fiery young radicals alike debated Garvey, Fanon, and Rodney as if they were kinfolk. Their words wrapped around him like the rhythm of the drums during Kumfaah ceremonies. At night, when the moon rose full and silver over the Demerara horizon, Michael would sit under the great kumakha tree with his cousins, listening to his uncles chanting folk songs that fused Alkebulan call-and-response with the new cadence of reggae. To him, it was clear: the old ways and the new sound were not in conflict; they were converging, forming a single river of awakening and resistance.

His awakening came in waves. At sixteen, he sneaked into Georgetown with his cousin Angella to hear Walter Rodney speak. The historian's words about the people's power to define themselves sent Michael's spirit quaking. "We are not what colonialism told us we are," Rodney thundered. "We are heirs of Alkebulan kings, queens, and warriors!" Sitting on the ground, pressed among other barefoot youths and university students alike, Michael felt Rodney's voice strike the same place in his chest where Marley's *Redemption Song* had taken root.

That night, he dreamed of Edna. Not as a dusty tale of the past, but alive; her eyes like embers, her braids thick as ropes of power, her arms spread wide as she led captives into the forest. She turned to him, and he knew without doubt: her blood pulsed in his veins, her fight was now his.

From then on, Michael carried himself differently. He walked through Kumakha not just as a boy growing into a man, but as a vessel of something ancient. The elders noticed. His grandfather, still strong in his eighties, whispered to him after a drumming session: "The fire you feel? That's your great ancestress, Edna. She is with you. Embrace her wholeheartedly."

By eighteen, Michael was both a scholar and a cultural warrior. He debated politics in Victoria Village, danced to reggae until dawn in Georgetown, and returned home to Kumakha for the ceremonies that tied him to the ancestors. Where others saw contradictions — between Black Power politics, Rastafari mysticism, and Kumakhan rites — Michael saw continuity. It was all one movement, one ancestral current flowing through different vessels.

Once, when he sat under the kumakha tree with a group of his cousins and friends, he declared, "Our story didn't end in chains, and it won't end in poverty. We are the continuation. We are the awakening." And in that moment, the circle of Edna's legacy closed and opened again, her bloodline igniting in the young man whose very birth had been marked as extraordinary.

FOURTEEN

Over the ensuing years, Rowena studied her son's every gesture and every word meticulously. She never told anyone—not even Vernon—what had transpired at Michael's birth. Outwardly, he was a normal boy, brimming with masculine energy, endlessly curious, eager to explore the world. But when Rowena looked into his eyes, steady and unflinching, she saw a depth of awareness that did not belong to his chronological years. Vernon, too, had sensed it. Half joking, half serious, he called his son "an old man in a child's body."

Michael's quick development was remarkable. Though five years younger, he was far ahead of his sister, Sheila, in nearly every way. She sought his help constantly, trusted his advice, and shadowed him as if he were the elder sibling. Sometimes she envied the way he lost himself in books, oblivious to everything around him.

"Where do you go when you're reading, Mickey?" she once asked, braiding his shoulder-length hair.

Rowena had entrusted the care of Michael's hair to Sheila, following the instruction of a dream in which her sixth maternal great-grandmother had appeared. The ancestor warned that cutting the child's hair would disrupt the magnetic frequencies that tethered him to other dimensions. So, Sheila became keeper of his locks.

"Even if I told you the truth," Michael said, amused but serious, "you wouldn't believe me."

"Please!" Sheila tugged playfully on his hair.

"Alright," he relented. "But promise it stays between us."

"I promise." She tilted his chin toward her, and he searched her eyes before speaking.

"I go into the places in the stories. I meet the people, laugh and cry with them, bury their dead, dance in their celebrations. Past, present, future — fiction and fact — they are all human inventions. The only boundaries that exist are the ones in our minds. Imagination frees us from them all."

Sheila cut him off quickly, uneasy yet fascinated. "Ok, ok. I know where you go now. Maybe I should read as much as you do — just to get away from this crazy world."

"You don't know what you're missing," Michael replied.

Sheila grew quiet, pondering his words. For the first time, she wondered if her brother's oddities were more than quirks. Their mother often spoke of genetic memory, the possibility that people inherit experiences from their ancestors. Could Michael be proof of it?

But Michael had already moved on. The rainy season was ending, and the garden needed tending. The kitchen garden, the fruit trees, even the yard; all of it fell under his care. That spring, he resolved to prune the black sage trees at the far end of the backyard.

At dawn on Sunday, Michael slipped downstairs, careful not to wake his family. He cooked himself plantain-flour porridge and two boiled eggs, ate in silence at the table, and watched the sunrise. The plan was to weed the entire backyard before the sun grew fierce. Yet something in the air felt different. A familiar tug of intuition stirred, his own quiet warning that something unseen was approaching. He dismissed it, cleared his plate, and stepped outside.

Whistling softly, he retrieved a machete and fork from the shed and walked to the farthest edge of the yard. The six weeks of rain had left the grass knee-high. The black sage cluster in the southeastern corner, ripe with berries, looked more like a thicket than ever. He had planned to leave it for last, but today his mind kept drifting toward it. He reached the trees and began clearing. Then he noticed something unusual. The ground beneath them was raised, like a mound. Curious, he cut with more determination, and the more he cut away, the more the formation extended.

"I'd never seen this before," he murmured. "This looks like a burial mound."

No ants, no signs of nests. He tapped the ground. It sounded hollow. Frowning, he laid down his tools and hurried back inside. Upstairs, Sheila was awake, reading her Bible.

"You look like you've seen a ghost," she teased upon seeing him in the doorway.

"Probably worse," he said. "Get dressed. Come help me pick the black sage berries. I think there's a tomb under those trees."

"A what?" she gasped, clutching his arm.

"Shhh. Don't wake Mommy and Daddy."

Minutes later, they were back in the yard. Sheila froze at the sight of the mound, then crossed herself. "Oh my God! How did that get here?"

"That's exactly what I want to know," Michael muttered.

After picking the berries, filling a whole basket, Michael dug into the mound's edge.

"Be careful!" Sheila warned. Just then, a sudden gust of wind swept through the backyard, stirring the animals in their pens. Brother and sister, planting their feet firmly in the ground, stared at each other, unsettled. The hair on Sheila's neck prickled. "I don't like this, Michael."

"Neither do I," he admitted, tightening his grip on the shovel. "But we have to find out what's down there." And with that, he drove the blade deeper into the earth.

FIFTEEN

Vernon and Rowena were now enjoying the fruit of their labor, their satisfaction evident in all they did. They had purchased the lot adjacent to the one they had originally leased from Aunt Drusilla — now passed on — and built a profitable mini-ranch with one of the finest houses in Kumakha. Their health was strong, their generosity abundant, and their affection for each other unmistakable. They still walked hand in hand wherever they went, carrying an air of accomplishment tempered by humility.

In time, all the skepticism and uncertainty that had once surrounded Rowena's decision to leave the Essequibo Coast and settle in a village none of her family had ever heard of vanished completely. Kumakha itself became a favored vacation spot for her relatives, who found themselves enchanted by its beauty and warmth. Ever the businesswoman and culinary genius, Rowena turned her home into a popular bed and breakfast.

The house itself was a marvel — one of Vernon's masterpieces. A two-story Victorian mini-mansion, its woodwork was carved with astonishing precision, its roof pitched at daring angles never seen in the region. Hexagonal turrets replaced the traditional cylindrical ones, and its wings and bays unfolded into a labyrinth so intricate that visitors sometimes lost their way without ever stepping outside. The saving grace was the wraparound porch, which circled the home and led to the front, side, and back doors.

Many of Rowena's relatives, upon returning home from their stay, could not stop speaking about what they called "the high culture of her people." Rumors spread that Rowena had been crowned "a real queen." And indeed, her transformation was nothing short of regal. She aged with grace and splendor: her long hair, streaked with gray, fell in ponytails down to her waist; her physique, compact and curvaceous, defied her years; her posture radiated confidence and self-assurance. Yet her most admired quality was her mind. She read voraciously; her intellect sharpened across disciplines like philosophy, history, and mysticism. With the bearing of a sage, she carried herself as though she had lived many lifetimes before, her love of knowledge matched only by her devotion to family.

When she had firmly established her foundation in Kumakha, Rowena brought her three older sons, whom she had left in the care of her parents on the Essequibo Coast, to join her. Basil, the youngest, was still a boy, while Berkeley and Patrick, the older two, were in their late teens. Handsome, industrious, and naturally talented with mechanical work, they both secured employment quickly, one in Peters Hall and the other in Houston, honing their skills in automotive repair. Like their stepfather, they preferred home-cooked meals, so Rowena rose early each morning to prepare food for them before they set off.

As the years passed and her older sons married, building families of their own, Rowena and Vernon entered a new chapter. With Vernon retired from construction, the bed and breakfast became Rowena's joy and her reason to continue rising before dawn. It was no longer just a business; it was a sanctuary, a cultural hub, and a living testament to the journey she and Vernon had taken together.

ROWENA, STILL IN THE HABIT of rising early, and Vernon, forever her quiet sentinel, had been lying awake when they heard Michael and Sheila whispering in the hallway. Without exchanging a word, the parents looked at each other and frowned. No footsteps followed; instead, the faint creak of the back door opening carried up to their room. Vernon slipped out of bed, crossed to the window overlooking the backyard, and parted the drapes just enough to peer through.

The sun had already risen above the eastern horizon, its warmth beginning to press against the glass. Below, he watched his children moving carefully between the black sage trees, picking berries with a sense of reverence. Their hushed movements and conspiratorial whispers stirred something deep in his memory. They must have discovered the earth mound, he thought. A flicker of unease ran through him. Could it be that the mound itself rises and falls with time?

Turning back, he expected to see Rowena watching as well, but to his surprise, she had drifted into sleep. A narrow band of sunlight slipped between the drapes and fell across her face, illuminating her features with an almost ethereal glow. She looked like a sleeping angel — serene, radiant, untouchable. Yet the sight jarred him. She lay exactly as she had years earlier, the morning he had found her collapsed at the foot of the stairs. The memory rushed back, vivid and unshakable.

As always, Rowena had risen before the rest of the household, lit her jug lamp, and gone downstairs to start cooking. Vernon remembered how, in that moment, she had been ambushed — how she had described a shadow darting past, someone blowing out her lamp, and then nothing. She had collapsed in the darkness. That morning, Vernon had sensed something wrong the instant he woke. The scent of smoke and food, Rowena's soft humming, were both absent. "Something is not right!" he cried, grabbing his jug lamp and racing from the bedroom. Berkley and Patrick, startled by his alarm, bolted after him, leaping down the stairs four treads at a time.

"Oh no!" Vernon gasped, dropping to his knees when he saw Rowena sprawled on the floor, face pale, froth at the corners of her mouth. He lifted her shoulders gently. "Ro! Ro, are you ok?" He turned to his stepsons. "Go get the Limacol, Patto!" he ordered, patting his wife's cheek. Patrick vanished and reappeared almost instantly with the opened bottle in hand. Though they were not his blood, the boys never once thought of Vernon as anything less than their father. He had rescued their mother, restored dignity to their family, and earned their devotion.

Vernon poured the mentholated lotion into his palm and held it beneath Rowena's nose. "Here! Breathe, love," he coaxed. Slowly, she stirred, inhaled, and moaned, the fog beginning to lift. "That's it. There you go!" Relief washed over him. "Let's take her back upstairs, sons."

"I'll carry her legs," Berkley offered, while Patrick took up the lamp. Together they bore her carefully up the stairs.

By mid-morning, Rowena had regained her strength, insisting with characteristic determination that she was fine. She brushed off the incident, claiming she must have missed a step and struck her head. "Y'all hurry on to work," she urged, slipping back into her matriarch's role. "Take some bread and corned beef just for today."

But even as she carried on with her tasks, something gnawed at her. She found her thoughts circling back, back to Leviah's piercing eyes, back to the strange cry Michael had made at birth, back to the apparition of pigs in the backyard when Basil had first arrived from Essequibo. Threads of mystery and omen seemed to weave themselves through her life, each one pulling tighter with time.

That evening, when Vernon and the older boys returned from work, they asked after her. "I'm feeling great," Rowena assured them, smiling. "Nothing hurts, at least." She ladled steaming portions of food onto plates, called for Basil, Sheila, and Michael, and set the table. "Y'all come eat some real food," she said warmly. And as they gathered, laughter mingling with the smell of dinner, the day's shadows seemed, for the moment, to recede.

SIXTEEN

Vernon lingered at the window, his memory gnawing at him as Michael and Sheila moved carefully around the black sage trees. He could see them whispering, their gestures deliberate, Sheila's body language betraying caution. He knew his daughter well enough to guess she was urging her brother to be careful. Still, Vernon did not intervene. He and Rowena had reared their children to question things, to seek their own truths, and he trusted their sense of responsibility.

But the sight of them digging at the mound rekindled an unease that he had carried for years. He remembered the morning Rowena collapsed at the foot of the stairs, the lamp blown out by something unseen. He remembered her frothing lips, the way her body went slack in his arms. For years, she had dismissed it as a missed step, as she put it. But Vernon, deep down, never truly believed it was that simple. There had been too many signs since they first moved onto this land — shadows, whispers, inexplicable moments that seemed to bleed through the veil between worlds.

Could it all be tied to the mound? he wondered. Had the ancestors buried not just bones, but memory itself, waiting for the right moment to be unearthed? He had often thought of digging it up, yet each time he hesitated; sometimes blaming the press of work; sometimes telling himself it was best left alone. But perhaps, he admitted, he had simply lacked the courage.

Now, watching his children take up the task, he felt a mix of apprehension and pride. Maybe it was meant to be them, not him. He made the sign of the cross and whispered, "Have mercy on them, Lord." Then, pulling the drapes shut, he turned away from the window.

Rowena lay sleeping, her hair falling in two ponytails across her chest. She looked so peaceful that Vernon was tempted to lean down and kiss her forehead, but he refrained. Instead, he tiptoed out of the room, padded down the stairs, and entered the kitchen. Moving quietly so as not to disturb the household, he brewed a cup of black coffee, then carried it to the dining table.

There, on the placemat, sat a small stack of books: his well-worn Bible, *The Gospel of Thomas*, and on top, a copy of *The Book of Enoch*, each marked with slips of paper for easy reference. Vernon stared at the pile, his thoughts heavy. A devout Catholic like his father, he had read all three from cover to cover, sometimes wondering if he had stumbled upon the apocryphal works by accident — or if he had been guided to them by forces unseen.

The timing of his reading *Enoch* had aligned too precisely with the dreams he had begun having. Dreams of demonic creatures — doglike, with fire in their eyes — chasing him through cane fields and even through his own home. Dreams of being seduced by a woman who, as they were about to embrace, transformed into a half-body, snarling, lunging at him with a dagger. In those dreams, he always felt hunted, always on the brink of annihilation.

And yet, there was one dream he could never shake. Cornered in a field, out of strength, he had dropped to his knees, arms crossed in the sign of the cross, chanting the 23rd Psalm. Just as the beasts closed in, a woman had appeared — an ancestor he did not know, dressed in all black, head to toe. With a staff raised high, she spoke words in a tongue he did not understand. Lightning cracked from her staff, striking the demons one by one until they dissolved into nothing. Vernon had woken drenched in sweat, heart pounding, but with a desperate longing for the dream to continue. Who was she? Which generation had she come from? How had she known to come?

He sipped his coffee, staring at the books but seeing instead Rowena's face the morning she collapsed, and remembered what she had eventually told him about Michael's cry at birth, which had chilled the midwife. The threads all seemed woven together: Rowena's episodes, the apparitions, the mound. Perhaps the answers had been here all along, buried beneath their feet. His children were outside now, digging where he had never dared. Vernon rose suddenly, the chair scraping softly against the floor, and strode to the back door.

UPSTAIRS, ROWENA STIRRED. She had just entered a dream of a long, dark hallway when the faint sound of a door shutting pulled her back. She froze, listening. For a moment she thought she was still dreaming. Then she realized the sound was real. She reached across the bed to throw her arms around Vernon, but found only an empty space.

Perplexed, she sat up and glanced around the room. He was gone. "Hmm," she murmured, head cocked, wondering what could have

94

broken their Sunday morning ritual. Pulling her nightgown tighter, she rose and walked to the window. Parting the drapes, she looked down at the yard below.

As if on cue, Vernon, Michael, and Sheila all turned their heads upward. Smiling, she waved, but the expressions on their faces betrayed more than casual activity. Following their gaze, Rowena saw that some of the black sage trees had been dug out and part of the mound laid bare. Her breath caught. Vernon had told her about it long ago.

Joining them, at first, she had condemned the idea of disturbing the mound. "Desecration," she had called it. But as the earth gave way to reveal what lay beneath, her intellectual hunger overcame her scruples. Among the relics unearthed were beads, tools, fragments of cloth, a dagger, and — most astonishing of all — a hand-bound, two-volume book with the title burned into its wooden cover:

Edna the Warrior Queen of Kumakha: 1713 – 1798

The papyrus pages glowed with exquisite calligraphy. Believing the ancestors themselves had guided them to this moment, the Byrnes reverently returned every artifact but the book to the tomb. Vernon rebuilt the mound, reinforcing it with a three-foot concrete wall so that it resembled a raised flower bed. The family kept their discovery secret. And in the quiet of their library, Vernon constructed a small altar with a locked glass case, within which the manuscript lay, waiting. Michael was the first to open its pages, the first to step into the epic of an Ashanti princess who had defied the Transatlantic Slave Trade and left for her descendants a living legacy of valor, fortitude, and grace.

PART TWO

ONE

The year 1717
The Asante Region
West Alkebulan

The death of our great and valorous ruler, the Asantehene, shook the Ashanti Empire to its very core. In just over a few decades, he had led us, the youngest group to emerge from the Akan Civilization, to great heights and prominence among the peoples of Western Alkebulan. Most of the coastal trade routes were under Ashanti control, and our armies, confident and valiant under the Asantehene, had begun an ambitious expansion along the coastlands. The aristocracy, especially the traders and merchants, had never felt any more secure than during his reign. Shortly following the announcement of his death, competing factions within the military started vying for power. Those loyal to the Asantehene wanted to preserve the union and limit the intervention and influence of the Arabs and Europeans, whom they realized did not have the best interest of the Ashanti people at heart. Given the fact that his territories abounded in gold, he decreed that all the gold mines became royal property, and gold dust be used as the currency of the empire. However, his adversaries, already corrupt by Arabian and European materialism and the wealth amassed from the Atlantic Slave Trade, and brainwashed by the doctrine of Islam and Christianity, sought leadership from "the pale race", as Alkebulans called the foreigners from across the desert and the ocean. Now, I must sadly admit a disturbing truth. My clan, though belonging to the same bloodline as the Asantehene, had aligned with the adversary group and, much to my disdain and disapproval, was very active in the sale of our fellow Alkebulans. So pompous and arrogant they were that I guess the table turning one day had never occurred to them. But unfortunately, it did, and that was how I ended up in this distant land called "The Demerara".

As legend has it, the roots of my clan trace all the way back to a Mande ruler who established the Mali Empire. It is said that he was born with an underdeveloped leg, which, to be precise, no one knew. Because, over the centuries, the oral account has shifted from left to right, right to left. Anyway, as a result of his physical uniqueness, he had been denied the throne. So, determined to let no one rob him of his birthright, he set out to improve himself through mindfulness, self-assurance, discipline, and arduous work. The first thing he did was to create a prosthesis. He cut a tree limb, which in turn had a ninety-degree protruding limb, trimmed the top of the main limb, above the protruding part, right below his knee, and the bottom part level with the ground. Then cut the protruding limb the same width as his foot, which he rested on that. Then, using a very strong and elastic vine, he reinforced the prosthesis and strapped it onto his own limb. Equipped with his spear and dagger, he would venture into the jungle alone and be gone for long periods at a time. In there, he meditated, prayed, communed with the ancestors and Ngewo (God), and exercised relentlessly, practicing spear and dagger fighting techniques. The fact that he always returned, alive, of course, suggested that he even fought and killed wild beasts not only for food, but to survive. Gradually, before the clans' eyes, he developed into a very strong, muscularly built, and commanding young man. It is said that most who faced him could not look him directly in the eyes, for the latter were blood-red and so spiritually powerful that he appeared supernatural. His stride, grace, and demeanor destroyed all disbelief in his ability to assume the throne, which was rightly his to begin with, and rendered him a true ruler, ordained by Ngewo.

Thus began the rise to rulership of the one remembered only as "King Tree Leg". Revered, respected, and acknowledged, he quickly mobilized the young men of his clan, organized and trained the best among them personally, then delegated the trained to form, train, and lead battalions. He commissioned all the blacksmiths, smelters, and other trade men to produce en masse spears, daggers, knives, and any other equipment necessary for an effective and successful army, exempting them from combat activities. Confident in the combat readiness of his army, he made his move and dethroned his cousin who had usurped the throne from him. However, it is worthy to note that, according to oral accounts, he did not declare himself king. He let his people do that. Once democratically secured at the helm, he began a massive expansion of his empire, with a focus on controlling the gold and salt trade routes to the Mediterranean Sea, which in turn allowed him to make education, research, scientific exploration, and agriculture top priorities. During his conquering missions, he would get many women pregnant but never failed in his responsibilities to his children and their mothers. He provided them with sufficient gold and salt to live beyond comfortably, got them the right social and political connections, and set many up in commerce and trade. It was during an incursion into the Black Volta territory and the Akan Forest that he met my eleventh great maternal grandmother, who became known solely as "The King's Madam". It is said that he was so smitten with her beauty, her charm and enamored of her that he ordered his men to build her own village, and that if she were to birth him a son, he would automatically become its first Odikro. Well, as fate would have it, she did birth him a son and later, a daughter; and his bloodline would continue down through the generations to my mother and the Asantene, her cousin. But my father, who had gained the bulk of his wealth and power from his family's commerce and trade, particularly in humans, did not like the Asantene, he forbade us from associating with him, supporting him, and even mentioning that we were related.

Unfortunately, however, wealth and power, especially that possessed by Alkebulans, did not guarantee absolute security against enslavement. From day immemorial, Alkebulans had been cursed with an irreconcilable and insurmountable tribal mentality, and the foreign invaders capitalized on this to conquer us. Not that they did not have their own tribal feuds, but in the face of survival and conquest, they learned to put their tribal differences aside and unite under one doctrine, either Christianity or Islam, as far as I knew. One of the qualities I have inherited from King Tree Leg is an insatiable thirst for knowledge, the resources of which have always been available to his descendants throughout the centuries. In addition to receiving books of all subjects and in various languages, thanks to my family's prominence in commerce and trade, in my early childhood, I had been assigned tutors in the Amharic, English, Arabic, Portugues, and Spanish languages, respectively. I became fluent in these foreign languages, along with Twi, Akan, and other Asante dialects. However, while I could have probably become a fitting ambassador of the burgeoning Ashanti Kingdom, I treasured an even more male-dominated vocation. Like my distant ancestors', my heart was with the spear, the dagger, and the arrow and bow. Accounts of our daring and victorious warrior ancestors in battles fascinated me; I could not get enough of their stories. When most girls my age were focused on the domestic arts and grooming themselves to become ideal brides, I was obsessed with breaking free from the mold. Thanks to the abundance of foreign literature in my family's library, I had read about the Egyptian female pharaohs, Sobekneferu and Hatshepsut, and Joan of Arc. Their lives and legacies fascinated me so much that I could no longer believe only men were born to be leaders and conquerors. Gender was not a determining factor in leadership. Guts, grit, and, as I had learned from Joan of Arc, a dose of ingenuity were the main qualities of a true leader.

I had my role model. I had the warrior spirit in my veins. I had the privilege and influence of belonging to a royal family. And I had the perfect plan to embark on my mission.

"WOW!" MICHAEL EXCLAIMED aloud, slowly closing the manuscript lying on the desk in front of him. He stared at it with a mixture of disbelief and awe. *What fate has led us to discover this treasure?* he wondered. *And why us?* Conditioned by his mother not to believe in coincidences and accidents, Michael was convinced that there was some sort of connection between this woman about whom he had just spent eight hours reading and his family. He was tempted to ignore the pang of hunger that was gnawing at his stomach and to continue reading. But just then, someone knocked on the library door. He got up reluctantly and went to see who was knocking.

"Hi Mom!" Michael said. Rowena smiled at her son, who was now a fully grown and handsome young man. "You have been locked up in this library all day," she said. "What is so fascinating about that manuscript?" Smiling, Michael took his mother by the arm. "Come, Mom. Let's go get something to eat and I will tell you all about it, even though I recommend you read the manuscript yourself. I strongly believe its content is very important to us. You talked a lot about genetic memory, and up until recently, I had still pondered the concept. However, having read the first few pages of that manuscript, I have begun to revisit your explanation of the phenomenon. The only thing is though, my understanding is not intellectual. Am I making sense?"

Rowena turned her head to the left and looked at her son, enveloped in an unfamiliar aura. "Well, as you already know, your mother is an ardent lover of our story. And sometimes, some of the things I read about don't seem to be mere discoveries, for want of a better word, but rather, memories, as though I were there — wherever *there* might have been —

witnessing the historical event. But let me not further complicate your mind. I will certainly read the manuscript when the time is right. In the meantime, let's nourish our stomachs. Eight hours without eating is a stretch. The food should be warm by now." Processing his mother's response, Michael smiled, and she reciprocated the gesture. "I'll be back down in a few minutes," he said, then turned and headed upstairs.

Rowena watched him ascend for a while before turning to go into the kitchen. She was proud of both of her children, and was amazed at how humble they remained as they grew into wonderful young people, well respected and adored in the village and beyond. Everyone said Michael was her carbon copy — in resemblance, temperament, and intelligence, along with a dose of her mystical inclination. Lately, since he had started dating a young woman from Peters Hall, she had seen very little of him. In addition, taking over the construction business from his father had kept him away enough, especially when he landed contracts in Essequibo and Berbice. She cherished his being at home, albeit locked away in the library for most of the day. And that, too, filled her with great satisfaction. Michael had also inherited her passion for reading, which explained why he could not wait to delve into the unearthed manuscript. The food was warm and ready: black-eyed peas cookup with curried hassah. As Rowena laid the table, she immediately missed her husband. Vernon was visiting his father's side of the family in the interior and would be gone for three weeks.

Michael came back downstairs and entered the dining room barefooted, dressed in a cream short sleeve cotton shirt and khaki short pants. Rowena looked at him and smiled. "I was just about to call you down," she said. Michael returned her smile and replied, "Well, the aroma did it for you, my dear mother, and here I am! We may…" Footsteps descending the stairs interrupted him from finishing his sentence. Wearing a pair of blue flip-flops, a blue jeans skirt, and a white tank top, Sheila entered the dining room and sneered at her brother. "I'm surprised you can still smell anything after being locked in the library all day with that … that—"

Rowena cleared her throat, and its dramatic effect was not lost on her daughter nor her son. Sheila zipped it and Michael followed suit, only smiling. Sheila pulled one of the two chairs at the head of the Mahogany table, which Vernon had built, and curtsied, "Si vous le pouvez, madame!" addressing her mother. Rowena obliged and settled into the seat. Michael pulled the chair closest to his mother on the right side of the table and gestured that his sister took a seat. "Thank you!" Sheila said. Then Michael walked around the table and sat opposite her, his mind racing back to young Edna in Kumasi, fluently speaking the Franco language. Might she have sounded just like Sheila? He wondered. Rowena took their hands and said, "Let's say grace." They bowed their heads in prayer. And right at that moment an idea occurred to Michael, and he toyed with it throughout the entire supper. They would be having a family reunion in December, which was only four months away. He would finish reading the manuscript way before then. So what could be the best way to share this saga of a woman whose journey, so far, seems to be nothing short of pure bravery and heroism, a woman whose legacy we are living? he asked himself. "A book!" He said aloud.

Shiela and Rowena looked at him with deep furrows on their foreheads. "Please don't tell me you're possessed by —
"

"Sheila," Rowena interjected, giving her daughter a stern look. Not the least embarrassed, Michael smiled and continued eating. Silence fell over the dining room, and it savored it to rekindle a thought that had lain dormant for quite some time. Having read so profusely and being so familiar with various writing styles, he had often toyed with the idea of writing a book of his own one day. *That day has come*, he told himself, and before supper was over, the book had already begun taking shape in gestation. When got back into the library, his typewriter became a time-traveling vehicle.

TWO

A single action can change the course of an individual or a people once and for all. This is exactly what happened when Edna, at the age of sixteen, woke up one morning in Kumasi, the heart of the Ashanti Kingdom, and embarked on a journey that she, perhaps, could not have imagined would be laced with even half the challenges, trials, and tribulations she would have to face, endure, and overcome so that this wonderful village of Kumakha could exist today and we all could be here, sharing her epic journey and legacy. This is the synthesized version of that journey, the story of a woman known only as Edna, the Warrior Queen. May her soul and the souls of those who deemed burying her manuscript with her fitting rest in eternal peace. Their action stands as testament to their knowledge of, and reverence for her as the extraordinary leader and visionary she was. As Edna wrote in one of her journal entries, which she labelled according to the cycles of the celestial elements, *"Full Moon — Who am I without the written word? And who will my descendants (if there should be any) be without it? Certainly not as complete as the sphere above that illuminates my path."* To conceal her identity and facilitate moving about freely under her disguise as a 'stunningly handsome young man' — a compliment she invariably got — Edna never mentioned her last name in any of her journals. During the civil disorder that had erupted following the death of the Asantehene, any relation to a royal family on either side of the political divide could have been reason enough to be kidnapped and, if not used as a bargaining tool for an exorbitant ransom, tortured and killed as an act of ultimate revenge. So, to which noble abusua, or clan, she belonged is not known, other than the fact that she belonged to a very powerful one.

The family's political and socioeconomic status was evident in its 20-acre compound, an architectural marvel of its era, which sat smack in the center of a 600-acre mocha coffee plantation, the first of its kind in Western Alkebulan. Built in the shape of an octagon, from the towering fortress of an outer fence wall made of stones and eight buildings laid out in the same octagonal pattern to the familial palace in the center, with its own fence wall, the compound resembled a medieval town with all the characteristic amenities. The palace itself, on which no expense was spared to reflect the sophisticated taste that its primary occupants had acquired from far and wide travels, boasted elaborately ornate doors on all eight sides and was surrounded by an inner octagonal stone wall, with the only difference from the outer wall being that this wall had two gates: one in front and one at the back; whereas, the outer wall had only one main gate, one main entrance. Each door led out to its own adjoining garden, manicured and adorned with fountains and life-size sculptures of Ashanti deities and mystical figures. The front of the palace, accentuated by intricately carved columns and facing the East, was accessed by a wide cobblestone walkway, flanked by busts of marble lions. Turrets with red mud-brick roofs crowned each point of the octagon on the walls and the palace, at the northwestern side of which Edna's chamber was located. As an extra measure of security, being that she was the only heiress, the garden adjoining her abode had its own fence wall, with a sentry posted at the gate twenty-four hours round the clock.

The sentry on guard four nights of the week just so happened to be Edna's favorite cousin, Ampah. Upon his birth, his father gave him this name as an honor unto the Chief, Edna's father. While on their way back from a trading expedition to the Abyssinia Kingdom, they were attacked by a group of caravan raiders, and in the midst of the ensuing battle, the Chief, risking his own life, had saved Ampah's father's life as the ultimate display of gratitude for the latter's trust and loyalty. In return, when Edna was born two years later, Ampah's father pledged him to the Chief as protector of the heiress. Thus, Ampah and Edna would grow up inseparably, often mistaken as twin brothers, for Edna was fond of dressing as a boy and indulging in all sorts

113

of physical activities that were considered primarily for her male peers. They studied under foreign tutors together. They ate breakfast, lunch, and dinner together. They perused the contents of the many books that entered the family's vast library — from the Coptic Ethiopian Bible, works by scholars from Timbuktu and Egypt to those of many Greek and Arabic philosophers. They studied the arts of spear and dagger fighting and archery together. By the time they became middle-aged teenagers, Ampah and Edna were so well read, so knowledgeable, and so versed in the defensive arts that they were enlisted as two of the top royal trainers of the Chief's personal security outfit. But most of all, they shared an exceptional level of consciousness regarding the horrific reality of human trafficking and slavery. The horrors of that infamous institution had penetrated practically every nook and cranny of many, if not most, Alkebulan tribes, particularly on the West Coast and in the northern part of the continent.

IN THE HEART OF THE Ashanti Kingdom during the 16th century, Ampah emerged as a remarkable young man, a symbol of noble lineage and profound consciousness. He was not only a prince, but also an astute thinker, gifted warrior, and staunch advocate for justice. His journey through life, marked by his education, valor, political awareness, and profound loyalty, is nothing short of a hero, a leader destined to leave a legacy. Born under the auspices of an Ashanti royal family, known for its rich culture and history of martial prowess, from a young age, he was immersed in the teachings of his ancestors, receiving a robust education that included the arts, history, warfare, diplomacy, and the traditional values instilled in him by the elders of the kingdom. His ability to absorb knowledge quickly set him apart from his peers, solidifying his reputation as one of the brightest minds among them. The kingdom's finest scholars, along with many from abroad, prepared him not only for leadership, but also for the complexities of the world around him. This education fostered an understanding of the political climate of the time, especially in light of the rising tensions brought on by European colonization and the horrific transatlantic slave trade. Ampah was particularly outspoken against these injustices, using his platform to rally support and raise awareness among his people.

Known for his striking handsomeness, with a commanding presence characterized by his tall stature and athletic build, Ampah was highly favored, particularly among the maidens. In his hands, the dagger and the spear were not merely instruments of war; they symbolized his commitment to defending his people and standing against oppression and slavery. Ampah led many successful campaigns against rival tribes and European intruders who threatened the sovereignty of his kingdom, and his skill in battle made him a celebrated warrior within the Ashanti ranks. Despite his prowess, he carried himself with an air of humility, treating his adversaries with respect when appropriate and honoring the codes of conduct that governed warfare.

The political machinations of the time, the growing demand for slaves in Europe and the Americas, and the subsequent raids on African villages disturbed him deeply. He understood that the enslavement of his people was a looming threat that could reshape the very fabric of Ashanti society. In gatherings and discussions, Ampah voiced his vehement opposition to the transatlantic slave trade. He implored his fellow royals to consider the dire impact such actions would have on their communities, families, and future generations. His arguments were bolstered by a profound moral conviction because Ampah recognized the inherent dignity of every individual, a belief deeply rooted in Ashanti culture. His perspective on the slave trade was born not only from compassion for his fellow Alkebulan, but also from a fear that he, too, could one day end up enslaved. He understood that the weakening of his people could invite external forces to exploit their resources and land. His foresight resonated with his advisors and fellow warriors, leading to increased caution among the Ashanti in dealing with European and Arab traders, thereby protecting their sovereignty. Despite his many accomplishments and qualities, Ampah remained grounded. His humility was a defining trait, endearing him to the common people and nobility alike. He frequently engaged with his community, listening to their concerns, and showing appreciation for their contributions to the kingdom's strength. True leadership in Ampah's view was not just about wielding power, but also about serving those under his care.

The most notable relationship in Ampah's life was his close friendship with Edna. She possessed the intelligence and wit that complemented his vision for a just society. Their bond transcended the conventional boundaries of friendship; it was strengthened by mutual respect, shared ideals, a deep understanding of their roles within the kingdom, and unspoken mutual love for each other.

Edna was a passionate advocate for the rights and education of women in Ashanti society, a cause that resonated with Ampah's own advocacy for justice. He supported her initiatives and often defended her against detractors who doubted her capabilities due to her gender. In fact, when she told him she wanted to disguise herself as a boy, as Joan of Arc did, Ampah enthusiastically assured her that the idea was marvelous. In return, Edna provided Ampah with insights and perspectives that enriched his tactical and political understanding. Together, they envisioned a future where the potential of every Ashanti was realized, regardless of social standing.

Their growth, however, was not without conflict, which would shape them into the individuals they would ultimately become. As Ampah approached adulthood, he faced numerous challenges that tested his values and resolve. The Ashanti Kingdom was not without its internal conflicts, and rival factions often vied for power, leading to a fractious political landscape. Ampah navigated these turbulent developments with a blend of diplomacy and martial prowess, forging alliances that strengthened his position and his commitment to a more equitable society.

THREE

efore heading off on one of the most ambitious trading expeditions of his life, the Chief Bsummoned Edna into his chamber to have a very serious talk with her regarding her ideological convictions and the serious consequences they could have. He had heard through the grapevine that "the princess", as everyone called her, was covertly campaigning against the slave trade. During the latter half of the eighteenth century, the Asante Empire became the most expansive and powerful state in the region. Its wealth and prosperity were based on mining and trading in gold and slaves, while its fame grew for its wood carvings, furniture, and revered Kente cloth. Earlier in the century, after waging wars of conquest, the Asantehene had conquered the neighboring states of Twifo, Wassa, and Aowin. The king who succeeded him led the integration of Akan states, including Tekyiman, Akyem, and Kwahu into the Asante Empire. With expansion came the need to develop a stronger and more powerful army. Thus, in exchange for European guns and goods, the Ashanti sold gold and slaves, who were usually captives of war or given as tribute from the peoples they conquered in battles. As the Ashanti Empire prospered economically, its culture flourished.

The bits and pieces of stories Edna had gleaned from various sources about the

120

atrocities meted out against the enslaved both broke her heart and hardened it at the same time. The princess was fully aware of all the risks and dangers that opposing such a profitable enterprise entailed, but she had made up her mind to face the consequences, including excommunication from her own family, or worse, death.

The chief was not of extraordinary physical stature, but the fierceness in his eyes and his aura made him appear like a giant, a man not likely to be pushed over.

The princess entered the chamber ceremoniously and stood before her father, Chief Adom, her heart ablaze with righteous fury. The sun streamed through the ornate windows of their grand chamber, casting pools of light on the richly decorated walls, but Edna felt a chill that no heat could dissipate.

"Father," she implored, her voice tremulous but defiant, "how can you even consider the trade of our own people for gold? How can you remain silent while our brothers and sisters are chained and stolen?" Her father's expression was unreadable, a mask of stoic expectation, anger boiling just beneath the surface.

"A true leader must do what is necessary," he replied, his words sharp as a dagger. "The kingdom thrives through trade. We cannot afford weakness."

Edna's heart broke at his pragmatism. The weight of her lineage pressed heavily upon her. With one last desperate look at her father, she spun on her heel and burst from the chamber, determination propelling her forward. She would not stand idly by while injustice marred her kingdom's honor.

Grabbing her twin daggers — gifts from her mother, forged from the metal of fallen stars — and her trusty bow and arrows, she raced through the lush, verdant paths of her homeland, heading toward the coast where she had learned a caravan laden with captured souls would soon pass. The air was thick with the scent of earth and foliage, but her mind was clouded with the image of her people in chains, their cries echoing in her heart.

After several hours of swift travel, Edna spotted the dust rising on the horizon, a telltale sign of the approaching caravan. Crouching low and moving with a silence honed by her years of training, she surveyed the scene — a line of captives tethered together, flanked by brutal guards; fear radiating from their eyes. She felt her pulse quicken, a mix of adrenaline and dread.

Drawing her daggers, she launched an assault from the tree line with the precision of a hawk. Arrows shot forth, each one finding its mark, and chaos erupted as the captors scrambled to defend themselves. Edna blended into the shadows, employing guerilla tactics learned through her training. She struck swiftly, disarming the guards and freeing a handful of captives, her spirit soaring with each life she saved.

The sun dipped low in the sky as the fight raged on. Edna fought relentlessly for nearly two hours, her body moving with strength and agility, but fatigue began to weigh heavily on her limbs. The determined princess was slowly losing her edge, her breath labored and her eyes dropping from exhaustion.

As she retreated with a small group of the rescued, bound by shared fear and hope, one of the captives — a young man, weak and delirious — collapsed in his tracks. Groaning, he pointed and gasped, "This way! Over here!"

It was a simple slip, but it was all it took. With a horrible crash of boots against the ground, the guards redoubled their efforts, encircling Edna and her flock. In their desperation, she fought bravely, but desperation breeds recklessness, and soon, she found herself overpowered, trapped amid the chaos.

With chains around her wrists and a sense of profound loss weighing heavy upon her heart, Edna was taken. She felt the eyes of her fellow captives upon her as she was led to the wagon, the foreboding shadow of the Cape Coast Castle looming ahead, known grimly as the Door of No Return.

The reality of her failure sank like a stone in her gut, but deep within, a flicker of hope still burned. Perhaps, this was not the end. Perhaps it was merely another turn in her journey, the Hero's Journey. Edna vowed silently to her fellow captives that she would not rest until every single one of them was free — and if this was the price she had to pay, then she would wear her chains with the same fierceness she had fought with.

As the caravan rumbled onward, the sun dipped below the horizon, the crimson glow, a fierce reminder of her indomitable spirit, undying even in the face of despair. The story of Edna, the warrior princess, was far from over.

Edna stumbled forward, her bare feet scraping against the rough earth, the unforgiving chains around her ankles sending jolts of pain through her body. Her wrists bore the raw ache of shackles linking her to the woman in front of her — an older woman with weary eyes and graying hair who looked like life had stripped her of dignity long ago. The reality of captivity was harsh and brutal. The heat of the sun beat down mercilessly, yet she felt a deeper chill within her. Death before dishonor echoed in her mind, a mantra that steadied her resolve.

As they approached Cape Coast Castle, dread pooled in her stomach like a stone. This was the destination for many — a place where hope was extinguished and freedom shattered. The slave traders barked orders, their voices crass and devoid of humanity, but Edna forced herself to block them out. She could not afford to be overwhelmed by fear or despair. Her survival depended on a clear mind and a steady heart.

Stay practical, Edna, she reminded herself. *You are not defeated yet. You are still breathing, still fighting.* Each step was a reminder that her spirit, although battered, was not broken. The girl who feared the wrath of her father and rebelled against compromising her principles had transformed into a woman of cunning and grit.

In the dank atmosphere of the dungeon that awaited them, dark stone walls dripped with moisture, carrying with them the stench of neglect and hopelessness. The air was thick with despair. Edna's eyes adjusted to the dim light, and she quickly scanned her surroundings, taking mental notes of every detail — guard patterns, the position of the iron bars, the cries of fellow captives echoing like a chilling symphony of sorrow.

Focus, she urged herself. *You are strong. You are a princess of the Ashanti, and they will not define you. Not today. Not ever.*

The woman before her, whom she would later come to know as Mama Akua, turned her head slightly, meeting Edna's gaze. There was an ember of understanding in the older woman's eyes, a silent acknowledgement that they were both caught in this hellish trap together. It inspired a flicker of hope.

"Mama Akua," Edna whispered, keeping her voice low, "have you any idea how many guards are on duty?"

"They are many, princess, but they are not invincible. They have overconfidence and cruelty on their side, but they underestimate our will to survive."

Edna's heart swelled with determination. If they were to escape, they would need a plan—a distraction, a means to regain their freedom. She could not rely solely on chance. Survival meant thinking strategically — a change that filled her with purpose.

Death before dishonor, she recited mentally. *If it must come to that, I will embrace it with dignity.* But she could sense the truth of Mama Akua's words. If a chance at life emerged, she would seize it with all her might.

Hours bled into one another in the suffocating darkness of the dungeon. Edna shared whispered stories with her fellow captives to keep their spirits buoyed, each tale weaving a fragile tapestry of resilience. Yet, her thoughts constantly returned to escape. An old, rusted window lay within reach, barely cloaked in shadow—but gaining access would require cunning and stealth.

With every passing hour, Edna's resolve hardened. She whispered to herself, *You are not a powerless victim; you are a warrior. Remember the techniques, the strength you possess. The moment will come when you can act.* The tales of her ancestors surged through her veins, empowering her with their legacy.

Through brief exchanges with Mama Akua, Edna learned of the structure of the guards' shifts — how they relaxed and became complacent under the spell of their own power. She would have to wait for the right moment — a time when their attention wavered.

As night fell outside, the cold seeped into the dungeon, and fear crept back into the hearts of the captives. Edna took a deep breath, forcing calm into the turmoil inside her. *Do not let them see your fear,* she thought fiercely. *Be ready. When the time comes, you will lead them to freedom.*

The first step would be to escape these chains. Edna's fingers brushed against the cold, unforgiving iron. Her wrists were raw, blood mingling with the dirt on her forearms, but she did not falter in her conviction. *I will find a way,* she vowed silently, the fire of rebellion igniting in her chest.

In that dank dungeon, bound yet resolute, Edna transformed her resignation into a fierce determination. She would not allow death to claim her without a fight, nor would she allow her spirit to be extinguished. The Door of No Return loomed ominously ahead, but she did not even think about what the consequences that lay beyond it could be. She had determined to not go through it alive or to make the ship a battlefield throughout the journey, where she would write the final chapter.

FOUR

Michael pulled the last sheet he had written off the printer and lay it face down on a stack in front of him. Retelling the story from Edna's notebooks felt like reliving it in person. He felt every blow, every excruciating pain, every sense of destruction and doom permeating every passing second. He felt it all, but strangely, not in his present body. Yet there was no mistaking what he felt. Even more paradoxically, he had remembered some of the scenes, as if he had not recreated them but lived them in another life. They seemed more than mere conjectures.

Anyway, hunger was starting to replace everything on his mind, for now, at least, and suddenly, he smelled the food his mother had just finished cooking. He turned the power on the computer off, stood up, and stretched, his muscles crackling under the pressure. Closing the library door behind him with a soft click, he went to the bathroom, washed his hands and face, and after drying them, he went into the dining room. His mom had left his supper covered with table towels on the dining room table. Michael called out for her a couple of times, but got no answer. She must be asleep or have gone out, he thought. Seeing the level of commitment and devotion he had put into preserving and making his ancestor's legacy accessible to her generations, Rowena could not be any prouder for having passed on to him her passion for knowledge, exploring and unearthing their story. Whenever he got wrapped up in writing, she would unplug the phone and often sneak out of the house to not interrupt him. Michael smiled and sat down to eat, his stomach growling with anticipation.

Midway through his meal, he heard the back door open, then he heard their voices. Rowena and Shiela infused the atmosphere with an energy that would pick the most tired person up and get him or her all attentive and curious. Shiela walked into the dining room, "Well look who is home from traveling back into time! It's my only brother, the chronicler of our ancestors!" She leaned over and planted a kiss on the crown of his head. Rowena entered and did the same thing. "Our timing is perfect," she said. "How is the writing going?"

Michael's mouth was full, so he put up a finger, indicating that she waited for a minute. He finished chewing and swallowing. "I'm actually surprising myself," he told her, looking up into her eyes. "In fact, I've started to believe that I am just a medium, and maybe Great Grandma Edna herself is retelling her story." Shiela chuckled. "There we go again, with this mystical stuff." She sighed, and pleaded, "God, have mercy on this young man." Then she exited the dining room and headed for the stairs.

"Don't pay your sister any mind," Rowena advised her son. She pulled her regular chair and sat down. She waited for him to finish chewing and swallowing the last bit of food that was on his plate. "Some things we just have to learn on our own. No matter what others say or do, if our minds and souls are not open and receptive to wisdom, which is far more complex than knowledge and understanding, we will never know who we truly are as humans. We will never connect with our divine essence, the core of our existence." Michael listened, not to find something to which he could reply, but to hear every word his mother spoke, to connect its meaning to what he was feeling. From his childhood, he had watched her go about life as if by pure intuition, guided by a force totally different from that which moved other mortals.

The phenomenon of genetic memorization suggests that the experiences, knowledge, and emotions of our ancestors could be encoded within our very DNA, influencing who we are in profound and subtle ways. This concept posits a deep connection between generations, where our inherited genetic material may carry more than just physical traits; it could contain the echoes of lived experiences and ancestral wisdom. This idea was taking shape in Michael's own life, especially through this writing process, and now through his mother's nurturing presence. For him, the act of writing served as a conduit for experience that transcends time and space. As he wrote, he felt transported back to the events of his ancestors, particularly Great Grandma Edna. He was right about what retelling the story from her notebooks felt like, a powerful and immersive experience, highlighting the visceral sensation of reliving moments long past through his creative process. Michael had tapped into a collective memory that resonated within him, allowing him to experience not only the facts, but also the emotions tied to his ancestors' struggles, triumphs, and everyday lives.

To him, his writing felt like a legacy being passed from one soul to another. A blurring of the lines between his own identity and that of Edna, embodying the notion that stories do not merely exist in the past; they can be reclaimed and experienced anew through the act of storytelling. Having felt like a medium, he now recognized the duality of his role — not just as a storyteller, but as a bridge across time, connecting the wisdom of the past with the understanding of the present. The act of writing also illuminated how memories can be deeply felt despite existing outside one's own direct experiences. The emotions Michael felt illustrated the weight of familial history, showing how these feelings can resonate within our own lives and shape our identities. Being a product of his lineage, Michael could not avoid invoking his ancestors' experiences, which lingered beneath the surface, activated in moments of reflection and creativity.

His mother, on the other hand, embodied the nurturing force that facilitates the connection between generations. Her pride in his dedication to documenting their family's story reflected a recognition of the profound value in such endeavors. Recognizing his monumental effort, she felt a sense of continuity, understanding how essential it was to pass down these stories to future generations. That was why she did everything possible to not interrupt his writing, demonstrating her deep understanding of the creative process. She recognized that true insight and connection often require solitude and focus. Through her support, she reinforced the idea that everyone's journey can serve as a vessel for greater truths, aligning with the concept of genetic memorization. By prioritizing her son's writing, she ensured that not only Michael's voice would be heard, but that Edna's narrative, too, maintained its resonance in the world.

Moreover, her conversations with Michael emphasized the importance of openness to wisdom beyond conventional knowledge, indicating that the pursuit of deeper understanding — of self, ancestry, and the human experience — requires a receptiveness to the wisdom that has circled through time. The knowledge of self, of who we are as a species, is crucial to our existence, Rowena taught Michael, highlighting how rediscovering ancestral knowledge entails both an intellectual exploration and a spiritual journey. As they sat at the table conversing, Michael and Rowena talked about the intertwining of inherited knowledge and personal experience. The tension between what is lived and what is remembered became a central theme in their discussion. While Michael engaged with the stories of Edna, Rowena reinforced the significance of emotional understanding as part of the narrative. Through Michael's retelling, the family story felt tangible; it became a living entity, rich with textures and depths that informed their collective identity.

However, Shiela exhibited skepticism toward his mystical notions of connection to the past. Thus, the back-and-forth conversation about his writing aspirations represented a dance between encouragement and a plea to be practical, a typical behavior in familial relationships with differing points of view. To keep his sanity intact through all this, he consoled himself in the knowledge that, in contrast, his mother, through her wisdom, advocated for an acceptance of the intangible. The implication through that duality pointed to a broader societal tension surrounding ancestral memory — where the sciences of genetics intersected with the more ethereal aspects of human existence. Striking Michael as very plausible, the concept of genetic memorization as a legacy seemed like energy, which could be transmitted regardless of time and distance. The profundity of the connections that threaded through the family stories and individual identity made him believe his mother was right. Stories — told and lived — shape our understanding of ourselves and our place in the continuum of generations, he concluded.

FIVE

Sensing her son was deep in thought, Rowena had stopped talking, allowing him the pleasure of rumination. Michael yawned, not out of boredom, but as a sign of submission to the weight of sleeplessness and wisdom. "You need to rest your mind for a while," his mother told him. "Great Grandma Edna would want you to be alert and perceptive, which you can't be, being tired." Michael stood up. "Well, I guess I'll call it an early night," he said, leaned over, and kissed her on the forehead. "I love you, Mom. Good night!" He turned, and as he exited the dining room, he whispered, "I love you, too, Great Grandma Edna. I'll be back with you tomorrow. Goodnight to you!"

Rowena watched her son walk toward the staircase and could not even begin to imagine what might be going through his mind. He had inherited her gift, no doubt, she silently acknowledged. Like her, he had the power to not just channel his ancestors, but to invoke the divine goddess, which he had done so from the moment he slid out of her womb. Rowena closed her eyes, and slowly, she recalled the first time she had heard the words he echoed at birth.

She felt the surge of energy resonate through her body, but still, she was trapped, held down by an unseen force. It wasn't just sleep paralysis; it was a mix of fear and the heavy blanket of the spiritual realm pressing in on her. As the thunder roared outside, vibrating through the air, a thought struck her like a lightning bolt — she needed help from Oshun, the Yoruba goddess of water, fertility, and love.

"Please, Oshun!" Rowena pleaded fiercely, her mind racing. "Grant me the courage to break free!" She envisioned the goddess, golden and vibrant, emerging from the strife of her dreams. Rowena had read of Oshun, a protector of women and children, and she yearned to feel that strength wash over her.

With a sudden clarity, she remembered the punt trench she had visited just days earlier, the one where she'd poured offerings of honey and sweet fruits, hoping to honor the goddess. Rowena conjured up that trench, its black water glistening under the sun, filled with light and life. It began as a whisper in her heart but grew louder, a call to her spirit.

Leviah, still chanting in the dimness, began to shift. The air thickened with the scent of oranges and honey — Oshun's essence. "Oshun," Rowena cried out in her mind again, "I invoke your name!" Her words filled the very fabric of her being, and she felt a flicker of energy rising within her.

Suddenly, the storm outside intensified, but now it was resonating in rhythm with her heartbeat.

The thunder became a drum, a call to action. Rowena concentrated, channels of her will focusing on each breath. She felt the weight of the paralysis waver as the power of her invocation swelled. The storm outside seemed to respond — a dance between chaos and harmony resonating within and without.

With all her might, she summoned the vivid imagery of black-water trenches flowing swiftly, their currents carrying away her fears. She drew strength from the vision of Oshun dancing upon the water's surface, anointed by the sun, radiating warmth and life. Rowena focused, channeling the energy through her heart, feeding it with her bravery and resolve.

"Arise, Rowena, my child," a deep, melodic voice echoed around her. It enveloped her like a soft breeze but carried the weight of the world. "Break the chains that bind you."

With clarity surging through her veins, Rowena pressed against the invisible hold. It was a surge of spirit and pouring devotion rattling against the chains of fear. She could see Leviah's lips moving faster now, chanting fervently, more than a mere incantation — it was a plea to the spirits to not release her.

But at that moment, as the storm reached its crescendo, a wave of golden light burst forth from Rowena's heart and surged outward. she felt the grip around her body unravel like threads of an old, worn tapestry. She gasped, drawing air deep into her lungs, the chains of impotence falling away as energy pulsed through her.

With a newfound strength, Rowena lunged forward, breaking through the confines of her paralysis. She bolted upright, shattering the veil that had trapped her in that nightmarish stasis. The garden came into view, the vivid colors splashed across her eyes like an artist's palette — the sun streamed through the trees, illuminating her world.

Leviah — a spectral figure now fading — looked upon her with reverence. "Ibè ni ẹ! (Blessed are you!), she whispered. "You have called on the strength within you," disappearing into the ether as the storm began to calm.

Rowena's heartbeat slowed to a steady rhythm, but her spirit soared. She would protect her children, her family, and herself fiercely, like the goddess she called upon. With a deep breath, she rose from the wooden bench, ready to embrace her life once more, knowing she carried a part of Oshun's courage within her. The world of light and possibility lay before her, and nothing would hold her back ever again.

Back from the reverie, Rowena looked at the stairs, seeing Michael ascending them, God only knowing what was going through his mind. She had not thought about Leviah in a very long time, which was good, she confessed to herself. Consumption in the wrong thoughts could be counter-productive, even detrimental. She had never underestimated the power of thoughts and words. She put much faith in them, yet she had surprised herself with the invocation of Oshun, especially with her staunch Christian upbringing. In fact, that had been a pivotal part of the fiercest internal battle that had been waging within her for years, letting go of indoctrination to open her soul to the spiritual awakening she was experiencing.

The phone started to ring, almost startling her. Rowena got up and went into the kitchen to answer it. Her whole being lit up. Vernon's voice to her soul was like fuel to a fire. The passage of the years, if anything, had only strengthened the passion between them. At a point in their life where many couples succumb to the weight of monotony and loss of that initial attraction to each other, they acted like teenagers freshly in love. Rowena turned and leaned her butt against the counter, her whole face flush with a beaming smile. "Hello, dear!" she whispered into the mouthpiece.

SIX

Edna blatantly stated in her notebooks that she would rather not reflect on the atrocities of the three-month journey across the Atlantic Ocean in the belly of 'that slave ship' — what she was conscious enough to remember, at least — except to say that she survived the "pure hell" only by the grace and protection of Asase Yaa, the earth goddess, protector of the treasures at the bottom of the ocean. For the first time in her life Edna had found herself not just in a servile but in powerless state, a state of helplessness and apparent doom. She had always known that she was a spiritual being experiencing a temporary physical manifestation, but she had never had the need to travel beyond the flesh — not until now.

THE belly of the slave ship was a tomb that had not closed yet. There was no sky, no sun — only the choking darkness of wood, sweat, excrement, and the quiet whimpers of the suffering and dying. In the dim light of a swaying lantern, Edna lay strapped to the floor, her back sore from the weight of chains and time. Each breath she took tasted of rusted iron and   despair.

And yet... there was a sound. The ocean. Its rhythm lapped at the wooden hull like a mother humming to her child. She had not noticed it at first. But as the lashes came harder, as the crew members grew more violent, as the shackled around her cried louder into the void, Edna began to hear it — the *song beneath the screams*. Not a sound, really. A *vibration*. A pulse. One night — or perhaps day, for time meant nothing in the darkness — Edna felt the foul breath of a sailor draw close. She knew what that meant. She had seen it happen. Heard it. The way women turned into sobbing husks. The way men wept in rage because they could not protect their sisters, their wives, their mothers.

But Edna... Edna had learned to listen.

Lap-lap-lap...
Ba-dum.   *Ba-dum.*
The sea's rhythm matched her heartbeat.

She closed her eyes. Her breath slowed. Her pulse slowed. Then she felt it: her *bones humming*. Her *soul rising*. A golden thread pulled from the center of her chest and spiraled upward, as if plucked by divine fingers.

Then — *stillness*.

When she opened her eyes again, she was no longer bound to her body. She hovered above it — saw the sailor's filthy hand reaching for her thigh. But he didn't touch *her*. He touched something else.

A *fossil.*

Her flesh had calcified into something ancient and inhuman. Cracked like dry earth. Cold like stone. The sailor gasped, stumbled backward, and collapsed, clutching himself as if something sacred had cursed his manhood.

Edna watched, calm as moonlight. Then the ocean opened. From the boards of the ship, water seeped in like mist. It did not wet the captives — it shimmered only for Edna. It gathered, swirled, became a portal, and from it rose Asase Yaa. Dark as fertile soil, clothed in leaves and waves, her hair braided with stars and roots, she extended her hand to Edna's spirit.

You are not theirs. You are mine. Come, child of Alkebulan. Let us walk where no chain may bind you, no unclean hand can touch you, said Asase Yaa.

And so they swam. Not through water, but through *memory*. Past sunken cities swallowed by time. Past bones of ancestors sleeping beneath coral blankets. The sea embraced her, and so did her heritage. Edna saw kingdoms that had once ruled the world. She saw queens anointed in gold. She saw warriors who rode lions and elephants and whispered to thunder. She saw that *she was them* — and they were *still alive* within her.

Each time a sailor approached Edna's slumbering body with wicked intent, Asase Yaa would appear. The ocean would whisper. And Edna's spirit would slip away, joining the goddess. The moment the man reached out, he'd see nothing but a hollow relic. Ancient. Dried. Dead. A husk unworthy of desire. His loins would shrivel, his breath catch, and his lust would vanish like smoke in a storm. Word spread among the crew.

"She's cursed."

"She's a ghost."

"She's watched by spirits."

"No man can take her."

And they were right. Edna was not the only one. Beneath her breath, she whispered the ancient names of Nyame, sky-father. Of Ogun, iron-bearer. Of Mawu-Lisa, balance incarnate. The gods of Alkebulan were not myths — they *lived in the marrow* of those who remembered.

And Edna remembered. They called her mad. Called her possessed. But at night, the other women would turn their heads toward her and whisper:

"Teach us, Princess."
"How do we, too, leave our bodies?"
"How do you escape this hell?"
And so Edna taught them — the ones who had enough faith in their gods and the spiritual fortitude to invoke them, along with their ancestors, aligning their souls with the rhythm of the sea, the heartbeat of the ancestors, issuing forth the chants that opened the soul's gates. One by one, they learned to slip their chains, even if only in spirit, to rise above pain. To become untouchable. They learned to rebel without swords and daggers.

Edna did not escape the ship — not yet. Her body stayed. But her mind and spirit moved through realms no white man could enter. Every visit with Asase Yaa carved symbols of power into her being. The strength of the lioness. The sight of the hawk. The patience of the baobab. She was becoming something else. A *vessel* for gods. A *conduit* for her people's rage and hope. A *warrior* of two worlds — body and spirit. She was not yet free, but unbroken.

In the darkness of the slave hold, where dozens withered into silence, one young woman lay still — eyes closed, skin calm. A sailor passed by her without looking. The others had warned him. "Don't touch that one. That's the witch. That's the fossil." Above her heart, faintly glowing beneath her skin, a symbol pulsed — an Adinkra glyph of strength. The gods had not abandoned their folk. They were only waiting. And Edna — *Edna was their answer.*

Bent over a huge wooden mortar, pounding dry kernel, she thought of Ampah, whom she had tried to block from her mind out of a sense of betrayal and shame. She should have consulted with him before she acted. She should have talked to him about her intentions. But she was afraid that he was going to stop her, discourage her from confronting the chief and, subsequently, going after the traffickers on her own. She just couldn't be stopped, and the one and only time she ever acted without his support, she landed herself in captivity. Now, thinking of him, where is he, she asked herself? Did he know what she had done and went looking for her? Did he, too, act out of anger, and ended up in the slave traders' dragnet? Edna thought about her father, too, and blamed him for all her troubles. Has he sent an army out to look for me? she asked herself again. Has it ever even crossed in his mind that I could have been captured all because of a system he has helped perpetuate? Edna fought back the anger boiling inside her and willed herself to stay focused on the moment. She had not survived torture, beatings, and dehumanization for nothing. They had stripped her of everything but her spirit, that inextinguishable fire that she had inherited from her ancestors, whom she invoked day and night and knew they joined forces with Asase Yaa to protect her.

The whispers came before the woman. Word of her spread like smoke on the trade winds — Edna, they called her. Untouchable. Marked by the old gods. Men said she made the virile limp, that any who dared lay hands on her were struck with madness, sickness, or worse. No overseer dared test the truth of it. When she had arrived in chains at Plantation Profit, on the East Bank along the Demerara River in Dutch Guiana, the legend had already rooted deep into the minds of all who beheld her. She was too beautiful to be flesh and bone, too still in her chains to be merely human. She was said to be protected by

Asase Yaa, a goddess of the earth — and the dead. The traders' records, clinical and cold, noted her as "disobedient," "defiant," "high intellect." But none of their ink could capture her essence, the eerie calm of her gaze, or the flicker of power that trembled in the air when she passed.

For four months, they kept her shackled to a rusting iron bed frame bolted to the floor of a windowless shack — alone. No light. No contact. But Edna was not broken. The solitude refined her senses. In the silence, she learned to hear the truth. Not words — truth. The pitch, rhythm, and sigh of a voice became scripture to her. She could unravel a man's soul from the cadence of his footsteps; divine his secrets from the way he swallowed his spit. The overseers, crude men who mistook their skin color for intelligence, spoke freely around her, assuming her mind was as blank as a starless night sky. They talked of routes and weapons, of the plantation's vulnerabilities. She filed it all away. Edna, the silent spirit, was listening.

But it was Charles Greavesande, the plantation's general manager, who drew her deepest attention — and who became her greatest study. Tall, robust, and rugged, he was feared across the colony. They said he delighted in mutilation

— one foot gone for attempting to run away. One hand for striking an overseer. His face was unremarkable. His voice was unmemorable — but his cruelty was the work of an artist. Yet in every monster lives a desire. And Charles's was women like Edna: willful, wild, unyielding. He saw them as conquests, and the joy for him was not in possession, but in breaking. He read the trader's notes with obsessive care. She was beautiful. Defiant. Educated, maybe. Dangerous, certainly. And so, he tried something different.

He ordered that no man touched her. Whether out of fear of her supposed curse or his own possessiveness, no one could say. He took her out of isolation, assigning her to his own kitchen. A test. A trap. He gave her her own sleeping quarters, complete with a real bed — a luxury by slave standards. And finally, in what he thought was a clever act, he began teaching her Dutch. He had no idea she already spoke his language better than most governors. And Edna played her part. Meek eyes. Soft hands. A quiet nod when he praised her diction. But in secret, she collected notebooks — any she could find. From Charles, from careless overseers, from the rubbish piles of the estate. Each became a vessel of revolution. She wrote down words, yes — but also maps, symbols, drawings of plants with poison in their leaves or sap that burned like lye. She watched the sky and recorded weather patterns. She documented which men hated the whip, which women hungered for vengeance. And with each center folio she tore from the notebooks Charles gifted her, she built her own books, sewn with strips of rag, inked with hope, fury, and the vision of free descendants, reclaiming the glory of Alkebulan generation after generation. And she wrote it all in English, just as an extra precaution in case her notebooks might be discovered.

By the time Charles began to feel something like affection for the strange woman with the endless eyes, Edna had already chosen her lieutenants. She had her maps, her allies, her plan. She knew which gate would be unguarded during the moon's third waning. She knew which horses would be unsaddled, what tranquilizer to give the tracking dogs to keep them under long enough for her and her army to vanish. She would not only escape. She would prove that slavery was just one chapter, one hurdle along the hero's journey.

SEVEN

Plantation owners and managers did everything possible to separate the enslaved from their tribal folk. Two people speaking the same dialect on a plantation constituted a recipe for rebellion. So, divide and conquer had metamorphosed into divide and control. However, due to the demand for numbers, physical separation was sometimes not feasible, and strict rules, or rather, orders, were laid down. Even close proximity of two people from the same tribe could have been punishable by public whipping or some other form of chastisement. That was common knowledge even when Edna was growing up. From very young ages she and her peers were schooled on the dos and don'ts in the event they should ever get caught in a raid. The ability to communicate with another person during captivity could be lifesaving.

Shortly after Edna was released from solitary confinement, a young man about her own age was taken to the plantation. The lacerations on his back were a testament to his rebellious spirit, even though he remained very calm and collected upon his arrival. Dark as a moonless night, he was of average height, muscularly built, and held his posture up with unmistakable pride regardless of his predicament. Edna watched him from the door to the kitchen of Charles' bungalow. As if he sensed her presence and gaze, the new arrival turned his head and saw her standing in the doorway, wiping her hands on an apron. They locked eyes, an intense wave of energy fusing their souls, and Edna immediately thought of Ampah. She felt a sense of kindred, an instant understanding and acknowledgment of the reason their paths were crossed. Without even batting an eye or uttering a single word, they sealed an unspoken covenant between them. They would not remain captive for long. Death before dishonor would become their motto. The fire in Edna's soul was rekindled. She turned slowly to resume her domestic chores, her mind racing through the plans she had already drawn.

EITHER CHARLES WAS TOO wrapped up in his ego and self-importance to notice that the arrival of his latest slave had disrupted the sense of complacency that had become too accepted, or the newly arrived and Edna were clever enough to keep things under wraps. Charles' main focus was on how much more the young man would boost his sugarcane production. He had bought him primarily for his knowledge of growing sugarcane, having been captured during a raid on his family's sugarcane plantation in São Tomé y Principe. Charles also liked the fact that the new arrival did not share any immediate tribal ties with any one on the plantation.

Over the ensuing months, Edna and the new arrival, whose name she learned was João, would find every conceivable pretext to get close to each other. They soon found out that they shared a very powerful weapon in common: they both spoke Portuguese. They would leave each other cryptic messages along paths they both walked, scrawled on a piece of wood here, on the ground there, or the less visible side of a tree trunk. After a while, their coded messages became so sophisticated that Edna began to plot their escape route in the cornrows she braided on certain recruits' heads. The fervor for freedom that they shared became such a powerful bonding force that neither could deny the attraction they felt for each other. On one occasion, Edna scrawled an ultimatum on a wooden plank that she knew João would fetch the following day, given that he was tasked with transferring a load of it from the docks to a designated location. "We must leave this place as planned. It's then or never. The inability to share with you more than just ideas and strategies of escape will send me insane faster than enslavement. Let's get the word out immediately!"

Then whispers began to spread on the plantation in the captives' own tongues, inspiring hope, laying out strategy, emphasizing the importance of timing. Edna and João tested their followers' courage, nudged them toward one another, and the plan began to breathe. At the end of October, the moon started to enter its darkest phase. A thick mist blanketed the night, challenging the perception of time, and Edna had chosen it for that very reason. She slipped from her quarters just after midnight and gave the signal for her allies to get moving. Knives hidden in sleeves, machetes in trousers legs, messages passing in silence, one by one, the key players moved into position.

The kitchen fire flared up higher than usual, the final signal the rebels were waiting for. The fire, however, was not fueled only by wood. This time, it was fueled by the records, the ledgers, the whips, and all the boots of the overseers. Everyone else, including Charles, was knocked out from the drinks laced with horse tranquilizer that was shared during a celebration earlier. The occasion was in honor of the Prince of Orange's birthday. While Edna went to the stables and fed all six horses food laced with enough poison to kill them within minutes, Joao went to the dog kennels and did the same. Eliminating the possibility of being tracked down was crucial to the success of their plan. With all the necessary bases covered and precaution taken, the two shepherds led their flock, each carrying a sack of provisions and other vital necessities, silently into the dark, guiding them toward the riverbank. Before getting into the boat, Edna counted the posse: seven women and six men. One man from the original lineup was missing. She turned to Joao alarmingly. He looked her deep in the eye, touching her arm reassuringly, and whispered, "I'll explain later. Let's get away from here first."

All the men paddled the boat about three miles up the river to a spot that had been marked by a unique tree that could not be missed even during the darkest night. They disembarked and pushed the vacant vessel out from the bank, leaving it to drift with the tide toward the ocean. The trek inward from the bank of the river was treacherous. Save for the usual sounds of the fauna, the night was silent. The canopy of treetops and thick clouds veiled the moon, cloaking the East Bank of the Demerara River in unrelenting black. The screech of a howler monkey echoed in the treetops, but otherwise, the forest pulsed normally, absorbing the footsteps, the fear, and the sense of freedom. Thirteen figures moved like shadows through the underbrush. Seven women, six men, each gripping a machete and bearing a sack stuffed with stolen cassava, dried plantain, salt, and smoked fish. Their feet were raw and blistered, their limbs marked by the whip and the work of the plantation. But their spirits were unbroken. Led by Edna at the head and watched over by Jocao in the rear, they paused from time to time to ascertain the direction of the wind, which was their only compass. At that time of the night, it was blowing northeasterly. One wrong turn and they could end up right whence they came. Edna's hair, once coiled and regal, now clung to her brow with sweat and rain. Her ears were trained on the sounds others would overlook — the hush of leaves, the pitch of crickets, the distant sigh of the breeze.

During a pause, she raised her hand and cocked her ear. Everyone held their breath and stared at her. Behind them, Plantation Profit slept. No one would discover their absence until morning, when the tranquilizer finally wore off. "We must cut this way now," Edna commanded, pointing with her left hand. "Let's follow the wind." Jomo, the tallest of the men, asked, "Which wind?" It wasn't a question of defiance. He just had a way of questioning even the most obvious things. Edna turned to look at him, then cocked her ear again up to the rustling canopy. "The one that protects us. Not the one that carries our scent. Let's get moving!"

And so, they moved, following her lead, pushing through the dark forest, trampling underbrush, breaking brambles in their path, using the machetes only when absolutely necessary. They weren't fleeing just whips. They were fleeing ghosts, memories, and the curse of never having owned their own names. The sacks on their backs thudded softly with each step. The journey improvised, with no map or physical compass, what they had was older: instinct, childhood memory of their native villages, and myth passed down from the ancestors through generations. They trudged through a tangle of bush so dense that even snakes didn't bother slithering through it. The scent of wild ginger mingled with the fetid odor of river mud. Twice they had to detour, once to avoid waking a sleeping caiman whose tail nearly tripped one of the women, and then through a thicket infested with bullet ants. They bore the stings in silence and kept on moving. Each mile was earned in blood, but it was blood worth shedding.

They took no torches. Fire was death. Instead, they followed the rhythm of the wind and the direction of moss on tree trunks. The latter nugget of wisdom was learned from Abeni, the youngest and smallest of them. Her maternal grandmother had once told her that parasitic plants used the wind to their advantage for survival.

At about two miles inward, they stumbled upon an old Arawak trail, nearly erased by time, but marked with a subtle pattern of broken twigs and stones shaped like crescent moons. It was a sacred path. There, their lungs burning, they paused to recharge. Blisters had opened on their heels. Mosquitoes feasted on their necks. But none of them cried out. Not even when Nia tripped over a root and nearly impaled her leg on her own machete. Nor when Kojo spotted the red gleam of a jaguar's eye, watching from the shadows. The cat sniffed the air, found no fear in it, and padded away. From there, they stopped only once more, at a stream so narrow it barely broke the surface of the earth, but with sweet water running in it. Edna dipped her fingers in, muttered a prayer to Asase Yaa, and smeared cool mud across her temples. The wilds of Guyana held their own dangers: bushmasters, vampire bats, quicksand pits, and cursed plants said to whisper in WaiWai dialect before someone vanished. But Edna knew all this: *Freedom does not come without stalking death.* And for now, they had eluded both overseers and jungle. "Drink only enough to quench your thirst," she advised. They had made it three miles into the jungle.

Even the forest whispered now. Not threats, but encouragement. Not despair, but hope. The rustle of leaves matched their breath. The wind carried their scent *away* from the river, not toward it. The animals of the Amazon, fierce and watchful, allowed them passage as if they too were accomplices in the escape. By morning, they would vanish, not just from the plantation, but from the known world. And the wind would carry their names forward, into legend. Behind them, Plantation Profit was waking to rage.

MORNING DAWNED ON THEM resting at the foot of a huge tree, with limbs so wide and leaves so thick that, upon them, one lying flat could not be seen from the ground. Knowing they would not be searched for beyond a certain distance from the plantation, given that no horse or dog was left alive, the group set about devising a plan to climb the tree without leaving any telltale signs. They scoured the area and found vines, of which they cut pieces of various lengths, some long enough to go around the circumference of the tree trunk, some short pieces to make a sort of foot clamp, and other pieces long enough to be joined together to reach from the ground to the treetop. Henry volunteered to be the first climber. He was Yoruba, about five eight, five nine, with a strong and lean body and a friendly but no-none-sense personality. After several attempts, Henry managed to reach the top of the tree, carrying one end of the rope. He secured that end to a solid limb, and then pulled the heaviest load they had up to the top. The rope held. Under other circumstances they probably would have cheered. But there was no time for that now. They looked at one another and nodded their heads.

"Amadou," called Joao to a humble but fearless young man, who listened carefully to learn, rather than to reply, and moved with deft efficiency. "You go on up now." Amadou nodded. "Sure, Sah," grabbed the vine loop, and did as told. "Now, we must ensure Madam Edna's safety above all else. The Madam, who was sitting on the ground, leaning against one side of the tree, sat up and was about to say something, but Jomo put up a hand. "Just this once, you have no say in this. Your safety lies in our hands." He walked over to her and extended a hand. "My pleasure," he said, bowing slightly. Being the supreme leader that she was, Edna knew it was necessary to step aside and let her king lead. She took his hand gracefully, and he helped her to her feet. For the first time since they left the plantation, she seemed conscious of herself. She dusted off her dress and allowed him to strap a harness around her waist and her ankles. He tested the knot. "How do you feel?" Edna looked him in the eye. "As secure as ever," she assured him. "Good," Joao said. "Then let's get you up there." He helped support her all the way that his reach would allow while Henry and Amadou pulled her up. "You're next, Nkechi," he informed the young woman who, he had noticed, stuck to Edna like a sworn aide and confidant. And in this manner, they pulled all the provisions, ponchos, tools, and the others to the top of the Kumakha tree, with Joao being the last to go up.

By now, they all spoke some form of a rudimentary common language, which would later become known as Creolese. Huddled in the treetop, they held council meetings and devised their plan for survival and moving forward. At the top of their list of priorities was the continuation of their genes, their bloodlines. Edna was the first to point out that risking their lives and all else would be useless without future generations. Thus, taking into consideration everyone's acknowledgement of that very crucial component of their mission, and being its supreme female leader, she chose one of the women as her sister-wife and declared their marriage to Joao, supreme male leader of the clan. Then she advised the remaining ten to pair up according to their attraction to each other. "Our tribal values," she asserted, switching to the various dialects whenever necessary, "are to be preserved and incorporated into the social and spiritual fabrics of our community. Never, under any circumstances, they should be reasons for distrust, dishonesty, disunity, and division among us. Any of those negative behaviors will be detrimental to our survival. Is that clearly understood?" Though the language barrier still posed among them a challenge for full comprehension, her authority and leadership needed no interpretation. They all nodded their heads up and down. "Very well," Edna said and turned to Joao. "Do you want to add anything, Chief?" Amadou paired up with Amaka, the chef extraordinaire among them. Like the odd couple, Henry, who now preferred to be called by his birthname – Khalil – and Adini paired up.

Chief Joao sat up straighter, his admiration and reverence for this fierce warrior queen

162

unequivocally evident in his every demeanor. "First, now that we are a little secured and relaxed, I want to commend you all for your bravery and your resolute actions." Edna interpreted. "Second, I completely agree with Madam Edna that we must reproduce to continue our bloodlines. However, I urge that we first ensure that our protection and defense are impenetrable. We are few, but always together, spiritually, mentally, and physically, we will remain strong and undefeated." The sister-wife, who had adamantly rejected the slave name of Jane and opted for her Igbo birth name, Nkechi, chanted, "Ase, ase," snapping her fingers. Others followed suit in their own dialects, and Joao allowed the spirit to prevail for a while. Then he continued, "We will follow the cycles of nature: the moon, the stars, the sun, and the rain. We are all familiar, more or less, with the forest, but we'll continue learning as we go along."

He allowed them to voice their opinions, offer suggestions, ideas, and even test the feasibility of one another's offerings. Then Joao said, "I would like to take this opportunity to make a confession, since I promised Madam Edna I would.

Everyone became silent and all eyes returned to him.

"I didn't mean for it to happen that way, but when you're leading souls through darkness, hesitation can be the death of them all. That night, as we prepared to slip away from the quarters and into the mangroves, I realized one of our men — Rico — had been whispering to the overseer's boy earlier that day. I caught the gleam of silver in his pocket, too — thirty pieces' worth, maybe not of silver, but of something close enough to buy a man's betrayal.

I knew the signs. His eyes couldn't meet mine, and when he did speak, it was with that forced calm of someone rehearsing deceit. He lingered near the storeroom longer than needed, and when he came out, his hands trembled — not from fear, but from choice. That was when I understood: if I didn't act, we'd be caught before the first oar touched water.

So, I set my mind. I told myself this wasn't murder — it was protection. A shepherd has to guard his flock, even if it means striking down the wolf wearing a sheep's hide.

I mixed the powder earlier that afternoon, hiding it in a flask of cassava brew. Rat poison —

bitter as sin itself. I told Rico it would steady his nerves, keep his stomach from turning during the crossing. He drank it with a shaky smile, thanking me for my kindness.

Within minutes, his breathing changed—slow at first, then shallow, then still. I held him until it was done. I whispered a prayer over his body before hiding it beneath the reeds. No one saw, except the stars—and they don't speak of such things.

When Edna noticed the missing man and turned those sharp eyes on me, I could feel the weight of what I'd done pressing on my chest. I met her gaze, steady but hollow, and said, "I'll explain later." Because how do you explain that the only way to keep us free was to sacrifice one of our own?

I don't expect forgiveness. Only understanding. Out there, freedom demands its price, and sometimes that price is paid in silence. That night, I paid it for all of us."

Edna met his eyes with an approving nod, and the silence that followed spoke much more than Joao had done, sealing the deed once and for all.

Over the ensuing two full-moon cycles, with the clan remaining mostly arboreal, especially the women, the foundation for what would become known as the only community of Alkebulans to have defied the institution of slavery and reclaimed their freedom in Guiana was laid.

EIGHT

Surviving the harsh conditions of the Amazon jungle was far more challenging than living through the horrors of slavery. Dealing with the weather increments without the benefits of tin-roofed wooden or brick shelters demanded pure ingenuity. Each member of the clandestine community was encouraged to tap into and fully exploit his or her special gifts, talents, skills, creativity, and even superstition. Necessity as the greatest teacher quickly manifested itself. Even though they had stolen all the boxes of matches they could lay their hands on, they had to use fire very sparingly and cleverly. Confident that they were safe, they began to settle around the kumakha tree, clearing the land, erecting thatch-roof log huts, irrigating fields from a nearby trench to plant the seeds they had stolen, and domesticating wild boars, turkeys, bush fowls, and other birds. Logic dictated that due to the density of the jungle, detecting smoke from even a mile away might have been unlikely, but they left nothing to chance. They dug a big hole in the ground and created a fire pit in it, and even then, they used it only when absolutely necessary.

Food could be prepared in many ways other than by fire.

With her extraordinary culinary gift, Amaka found the most creative ways to prepare meals from anything edible that nature provided. As if ordained by Apolo himself, shafts of sunlight beamed down through openings in the canopy of leaves. Amaka and her assistant, Thandeka, dried provisions of all sorts in the sun. The two women, both medium built and charcoal dark, went about their duties as if they were automatedly synchronized. Seldom talking to each other verbally as they worked, Amaka the bustier of the two, they shared an ancient wisdom of nutrition and sustenance that was unmistakable to the palate. In addition to her own passion for cooking, Thandeka also had a knack for herbal medicine. Within months of foraging the forest surrounding their settlement, she had discovered a plethora of remedies, cures, and therapies for both humans and crops. On order from Edna, she had discontinued administering birth-control syrup to all the women of the clan, and within the first month afterward, Adini, Amaka, and Edna herself became pregnant. "Sister Oko" everyone soon started calling her, invoking the Yoruba god of agriculture and fertility.

168

While Amaka and Thandeka kept the clan well fed, nourished, and healthy, Joao, Khalil, Chiedza, and Amadou tended to the farm, rotating and keeping it flourishing year-round. Jomo, the master builder who had designed the layout of the village, naturally assumed the responsibility of community maintenance and expansion. Nommo, a Dogon and the most eccentric of them all, provided updates on the patterns of the weather and the cycles of the moon and the sun and the stars. Fondly nicknamed "the moongaser", he spent most of his time buried in unraveling theories and hypotheses of science and mathematics, and was also appointed the trusted scout by the community council. His pairing up with Ziyanda, a self-proclaimed — and often proven — mystic, attested to the saying that opposites attract. She was forever seeking direct, personal experience or union with the divine, the sacred, the ultimate reality through inner contemplation, spiritual practices, and altered states of consciousness. Unlike Nommo, for whom conventional understanding and logic were paramount, Ziyanda relied on pure intuition and deep inner knowing. She had a strong distrust for doctrine, especially Christianity and Islam. Always wearing a unique headwrap and adorned with beaded necklaces and bracelets, her sacred amulets, as she preferred to call her adornments, she claimed to receive insights from the cosmos through meditation, solitude, and a profound sense of connection to the Creator.

The day marked one full cycle of the sun since their arrival beneath the sacred Kumakha tree, where roots coiled like serpents guarding ancient secrets and branches stretched skyward like arms in prayer. A year of survival, a year of building, a year of believing they had finally found sanctuary.

Edna, though deeply tied to the rhythms of motherhood and the duties of domestic life, could not surrender the fire that still burned in her mid-twenties' veins. Her spirit, sharpened on ships of misery and fields of bondage, refused to dim. She rose with the dawn, spear in hand, her silhouette cutting against the gold of the horizon. The others whispered she was more than a woman — she was a vessel of Asase Yaa, chosen to shield them when darkness prowled.

Nkechi, steady as the river that nourished their land, balanced her sister-wife's flame with calm resolve. Where Edna embodied the storm, Nkechi was the fertile soil that caught the rain.

She led the women in weaving, cooking, teaching the children, and tending the sacred fire at the heart of the settlement. But she, too, had inherited the bloodline of warriors, and when Edna called, she answered without hesitation.

Together they trained in secret, their movements precise and fluid, twin shadows dancing beneath the ancient tree. Edna, quick and fierce, struck with the ferocity of a hawk, while Nkechi, deliberate and patient, parried like the tortoise — unyielding and calculated. The younger ones gathered in awe, watching, learning, whispering that these two were not merely women but living testaments to the gods' promise.

Joao ruled as leader, revered and respected, but even he knew that Edna's mind was the forge where strategy was tempered. His strength was the pillar, yet her vision was the map. Nkechi reinforced that vision, anchoring it in the fabric of daily life, ensuring that no dream of freedom unraveled into chaos.

And so, on that morning of the three hundred and sixty-fifth rising, as the community celebrated their endurance with chants and offerings to the ancestors, Edna and Nkechi stood side by side. Not only wives, not only mothers, but guardians — sister wives from

171

Heaven, bound by duty, spirit, and an unspoken vow that safety could never breed complacency. For Edna felt it stirring in her bones: a test was coming.

NINE

The dawn of the one thousandth and ninety-fifth sunrise should have been one of celebration. The Kumakha tree, towering sentinel of their sanctuary, shimmered in the morning haze as if the ancestors themselves had polished its bark overnight. Songs rose among the women. Children clapped their hands, and men tended to the fire with renewed hope. Three years free. Three years unbroken.

But Edna could not shake the unease in her spirit. She rose from her mat before the first bird had sung, her eyes scanning the forest's edge. The air itself seemed to whisper warning, carrying scents of iron and smoke unfamiliar to their refuge. She felt it in her bones — the way warriors sense the coming of war before the first arrow   flies.

"Restless?" Nkechi's voice came softly behind her. She cradled her infant son against her hip, eyes calm but watchful.

"The forest stirs differently today," Edna replied, her gaze fixed eastward. "The gods do not let me rest. Something moves toward us."

Nkechi pressed her lips together. She had learned to trust Edna's instincts, for they had never failed. When others laughed at the younger wife's visions, Nkechi remembered the ship, the plantation, the escapes that had seemed impossible but had unfolded exactly as Edna foretold.

By midmorning, Nommo, the scout, burst into the clearing, his chest heaving, eyes wide with terror. "Soldiers!" he gasped. "Colonial soldiers, marching along the bank of the Lamaha canal. And not alone. They travel with the Carib headhunters — painted, armed with blowpipes and clubs."

The women faltered in their songs. The children fell silent. Even Joao, broad-shouldered and commanding, clenched his jaw in sudden gravity. The celebration shifted to dread in a single   breath.

"They've discovered us," Joao muttered. "After three years, they've finally tracked us here."

"Maybe not quite yet," the scout said. "But I was at the water's edge when I heard their voice some distance away. So I moved inward, far enough to where they could not see me, but close enough to be able to observe them. They seemed intent on sticking to the bank of the Lamaha.   "

"But if the headhunters had picked up your scent, they could well have changed direction," reasoned Khalil.

Edna stepped forward, her spear, which hardly ever left her side, gleaming in the filtered sunlight. "Then they come to test our worth. Do you think the gods would grant us this sanctuary without asking us to defend it?" Her voice cut through the murmurs like a blade.

A few of the men bowed their heads, others shuffled their feet, fear gnawing at their resolve. The mention of Amerindian headhunters struck terror deeper than the soldiers — their reputation for swift ambushes and decapitated trophies was legend.

Edna lifted her chin. "If you tremble, tremble now. But tomorrow, you will stand. No enemy takes our lives, our children, our future, without meeting the wrath of this community. Not while I breathe."

Joao studied her, the weight of leadership pressing on his shoulders. Though he was acknowledged as supreme leader, he knew the flame that kept their people from despair burned in Edna's chest. "Then speak, my Queen. Tell us what must be done."

She strode beneath the vast branches of the Kumakha tree, her voice rising with the authority of one possessed by the goddess herself.

"We will not cower in huts waiting to be

slaughtered. We fight on the ground of our choosing. The Lamaha will be their path, but it will also be their grave. Tonight, we sharpen our spears, daggers, and arrows. Tonight, we set snares where the forest narrows. If indeed, as Khalil believes, they have followed Nommo, then we know where to intercept them – and eliminate them before they can even blink. Tonight, all but Ziyanda and the children will march eastward. My sisters, you must hold fast as warriors beside our men – our kings!"

The crowd stirred, their fear transforming into the first sparks of courage. Nkechi, her child now at her breast, nodded fiercely and spoke on behalf of the other women. "Steadfast we are. No threat comes close to children. NEVER!"

At this, Edna's eyes softened. Sister-wife, balance, soil and water to her flame. Together they formed the core of their people's survival. All that day, the Kumakha village was alive with preparation. Spears were honed, bows strung, pits dug and camouflaged with leaves. Ziyanda and the children practiced hiding at the first sounds of imminent danger. Drums beat low and steady, the heartbeat of a people reminding themselves that fear could be transformed into rhythm, into strength.

Edna moved among her people,

touching shoulders, whispering encouragement, correcting stances, reinforcing the efficiency of thrusting instead of swinging in close combat. To each she gave not only instruction but belief: "You are chosen. You are strong. You made through the doors of Hell and across the ocean in the bellies of slave ships because you are the descendants of those who would not be broken."

At the edge of the village, she paused to gaze beyond the tree line where darkness thickened. Her spirit reached upward to the goddess Asase Yaa, and then downward to the restless souls of the ancestors. "Give me sight. Give me strength. Give me cunning," she prayed. "For they come not only to kill us, but to erase us. And that, I will never allow." The night air answered with silence, yet in her chest burned the certainty of divine companionship. For one last time, she inspected her anxious warriors, ready to stop the hovering threat once and for all. Edna gripped her spear, her eyes gleaming with the fire of defiance as she turned to her people, her voice steady and thunderous. "The gods have delivered us and granted us three years of freedom, and in that time we have created a new generation. Now we must prove we deserve such privilege. Let's go!" As they moved away from the sacred tree, the warriors of the hidden community were prepared to meet death with unyielding life.

TEN

The forest swallowed them in silence. Edna crouched low beneath a tangle of roots, every nerve sharpened to the pulse of the earth. Her warriors moved like shadows around her — men and women alike, faces streaked with ash and crushed leaves, their breaths steady, their eyes intent. The Kumakha tree still stood tall behind them, guardian of their sanctuary, but Edna knew safety was not found in retreat. Safety was earned in blood and vigilance.

She had chosen this place with care. A narrow bend in the canal where the soldiers and their Amerindian allies would be forced to march close together, hemmed by steep banks and dense undergrowth. It was here the intruders would be blinded, their muskets heavy and slow, their confidence turned against them.

"Khalil," Edna whispered, signaling to the lanky youth crouched at her side. His bow was strung, his hands trembling only slightly. "Eyes on the ridge. If they break formation, call the signal."

"Yes, Mama Edna," he whispered back, determination outweighing his fear.

The waiting was always the hardest. The forest seemed to hold its breath with them. Hours passed in the rhythm of night owls and distant bird calls. Sweat ran down spines. Knees cramped. But Edna's eyes never left the shadowed path.

Then came the sound — faint at first, then swelling into the distinct cadence of boots striking earth. Muskets clanked against belts, voices muttered in harsh European tones, followed by the guttural laughter of the Carib mercenaries.

Edna raised her hand. Her warriors tensed, bows drawn, spears angled forward.

The column emerged, five figures moving in a staggered line: three soldiers in red, their coats dirtied by the march, bayonets gleaming even in shadow; and two headhunters, bodies painted with swirls of crimson and white, hair braided with feathers, eyes alert and cruel.

They thought themselves hunters.

Edna smiled coldly.

At her signal, a shower of arrows rained from the ridge. One soldier dropped instantly, an arrow buried in his throat. The others stumbled, shouting, raising muskets too slowly against an enemy they could not see.

The Caribs lunged toward the trees, blowpipes raised, but Edna was already moving. She leapt from her hiding place with a cry that pierced the canopy, her spear striking the first headhunter in the gut. The man folded, stunned by her ferocity, before her blade ripped upward, silencing him forever.

The other warriors erupted from the undergrowth, their voices a storm, their blades flashing. Panic shattered the intruders' cohesion. A musket discharged wildly, the ball hitting Khalil's shoulder and spinning him backward. Hissing in pain, scrambled to his feet, clutching his bow with his uninjured hand.

The second headhunter charged, teeth bared, spear raised high, rushed toward Khalil, but Edna was on him. He snarled in her face. For a heartbeat they grappled, strength against strength, until she shifted her weight, twisted, and snapped his neck with a brutal thrust of her dagger. His body fell at her feet.

The remaining two soldiers tried to retreat, but the warriors had them surrounded. Spears struck from every side. One man screamed as his leg was impaled and dragged beneath him. The last one fought valiantly, bayonet slashing, but the numbers overwhelmed him. Edna ended it cleanly, her dagger piercing his heart.

Then came silence. Only the canal spoke, carrying away the echoes of violence with its rushing tide.

Edna wiped her blade clean on a soldier's coat, her chest rising and falling with the controlled breath of one who had embraced her destiny. She turned to her people. Khalil was already being tended to by Nkechi, who pressed cloth to his wound, her voice soothing even as her eyes burned with pride.

"You will live, King," Nkechi said firmly. "The gods have spared you."

Edna nodded. She looked down at the five lifeless bodies sprawled across the ground. "Leave no trace," she commanded. "Cut them apart. Let the forest take what it will. By dawn, there must be nothing left for their masters to follow."

It was done quickly and without ceremony. Blades flashed, flesh parted, and the remains were scattered where scavengers would finish the work. No grave, no monument — only bones to be swallowed by earth and beast.

When the ultimate erasure was finished, Edna raised her clean dagger to the canopy. Her people followed suit, voices rising in a chant older than memory.

"This is the price of freedom," she declared. "And it will not be the last. They will come again. But so will we. Always."

The chant rolled like thunder through the trees, carrying with it not just victory but a warning.

For the first time since their arrival beneath the Kumakha tree, the community had struck first — and struck with such finality that the forest itself seemed to acknowledge them as its true heirs.

And though Khalil's blood had stained the soil, Edna's heart blazed with the certainty of what the ancestors demanded: vigilance, unity, and unrelenting war against those who would see them enslaved.

ELEVEN

Gradually, as the years after *The Ambush of the Headhunters* went by, life around the Kumakha tree settled into an almost deceptive rhythm of peace. The bloody clash that had once defined their unity became less a warning and more a story told by firelight, a tale meant to awe the children and stir pride among the elders. The constant state of high alert that had once marked their days — scouts at the edge of the forest, drills in the clearing, women armed with spears, daggers, and arrows and bows while pounding cassava — began to fade.

First, the scouts, some now as young as early teens, returned less often with news of the outside world. "The soldiers will not come back," they said with a shrug, their confidence growing bolder with each quiet season. Eventually, one year passed without a single reconnaissance trip. Then two. The underbrush swallowed the narrow paths once used for patrol, and the forest grew wild in places where the feet of vigilant men had once trimmed it back.

The hiding drills, once so strict that even the smallest child knew which hollow log or woven mat would conceal them, became fewer and fewer. What had once been a weekly rhythm — drop the basket, grab the spear, scoot into the trees in a well-choreographed manner maneuver — became a rare practice. And when the drills did happen, the younger children laughed, more excited by the game of chase than the gravity of survival.

Even the defense training, once sharpened to the edge of necessity, began to dull. Spears leaned longer against the walls of huts; bows were left unstrung until hunting demanded them. Warriors who had once moved like shadows through the night became slower, more accustomed to rest than readiness.

Life, instead, swelled in other ways. The community grew. Children became teenagers, their voices cracking, their limbs stretching taller with every moon. Teenagers became young adults, full of pride and mischief, restless to test themselves in ways that did not involve silent waiting in the trees. Babies were born year after year, swelling the village with laughter, with mischief, with the endless questions of youth.

The bonfires grew bigger with each season. What had once been modest gatherings became great celebrations, their flames licking high into the star-studded sky. Drums thundered, dances lasted until dawn, and voices raised songs of freedom that carried far into the forest night.

But even as youth surged, age made its quiet mark. The founding fathers and mothers — the ones who had fled the plantation, who had built the first shelters beneath the Kumakha — began to carry the weight of years. Gray hair gleamed in the firelight where once black braids had shone. Strong backs bent, steps slowed, and eyes that had once pierced the dark faltered, clouded by age. One woman leaned always on her daughter's arm. Another man's hands shook too much to carve wood as he once had. And among them was the first whose body betrayed him completely: stiffened joints, twisted with arthritis, leaving him immobile and bound to the hammock where others tended his needs.

And then came the first death.

It was Khalil. The seasoned warrior who had bled during the ambush. The man who had refused to let his wound keep him from the hunt, from laughter, from the duties of a man. His shoulder had healed, yes — but never his spirit.

Shadows clung to him. Loud noises startled him. He avoided the crack of firewood and the sharp clash of metal. His eyes clouded by memories only he could see. Years passed, but the shot that had marked him on that fateful day marked him deeper than flesh. When his time came, it came quietly, like the slipping away of a tide. One morning, the sun rose, and Khalil did not.

The news rippled through the community with the shock of inevitability. No one had yet crossed the threshold into the realm of the ancestors. No one had dared to imagine that the Kumakha people — so strong, so blessed, so protected — could lose one of their own. But here it was: the truth that even freedom does not save a body from mortality.

The Burial Ground had already been chosen, though until that day it had been only a patch of earth whispered about, pointed to, and left untouched. But then it became hallowed. Khalil's funeral stretched three days and three nights, a ceremony befitting a fallen prince. Drums pounded through the hours, sometimes slow as a heartbeat, sometimes fierce as a storm. Women keened, their voices rising to pierce the heavens, carrying his name to the ancestors. Warriors stood guard around the fire, spears crossed in solemn salute. Children brought offerings of woven mats, gourds of cassava drink, carved toys he had once given them.

Edna herself spoke at the pyre, her voice steady though her heart ached with the weight of memory. "He was the first to bleed for us," she said. "The first to remind us that freedom is costly. And though his wound never left him, neither did his courage. He walks now with the ancestors, and they will know him by his scar."

When the body was lowered into the earth, the community covered him not only with soil but with prayers, songs, and promises. Promises that they would remember. Promises that they would not let complacency betray the sacrifices of those who came before.

And yet, even as the last ember of the funeral fire dimmed, Edna felt the truth gnawing at her. The Kumakha had grown strong, yes — but also soft. Too many spears dulled. Too many eyes looked only inward. Khalil's death was not just the loss of a man. It was a warning. And though few heard it, Edna did.

TWELVE

Seasons had turned since Khalil's burial, yet the unease in Edna's chest never quieted. She rose before dawn each day, walking the perimeter of the settlement, her dagger still sharp, her eyes still keen. To her, the forest was never just birdsong and silence — it was a veil, behind which danger could wait with patient teeth.

But not everyone agreed.

"Your eyes see shadows where there are none," one of her sons scoffed as she corrected his spear stance during a half-hearted drill. "No soldiers have come in years, Queen Mother. No headhunters. Why train as if ghosts still hunt us?"

Laughter followed, not cruel, but dismissive. The younger ones carried themselves with the confidence of those who had never truly known chains, never felt the lash of the overseer. They were born beneath the shade of the great and sacred Kumakha tree, reared in freedom, and to them vigilance tasted too much like fear.

Even Joao, Edna's anchor through so many trials, began to push back. One night, as Edna urged him to rejoin the defense circle, he sighed and leaned heavily on his staff.

"My bones are too old for battle, Edna," he muttered. "The gods know I have given enough. My strength is for leading now, not fighting."

"Then lead them to readiness," she retorted, her voice sharp. "What good is a leader who tells his people to sleep while wolves circle the fire?"

Joao's tired eyes softened with both love and weariness. "And what good is a wife who drives her people to exhaustion fighting shadows? Must every rustle of leaves be war in your heart?" The words cut, for they came not from malice but from fatigue — the fatigue of a man who longed for peace in his final years. Yet Edna's spirit burned against his resignation. She would not let the people forget the price of their freedom, even if it meant standing alone.

And then the signs appeared.

Footprints near the bank of the canal. Ash from a fire not their own. The faint echo of voices carried on the wind, voices speaking neither the clipped tones of the colonials nor the guttural chants of the Caribs. These were different tones. Similar to theirs in many ways.

Edna's alarm spread quickly. Drums called the village militia to arms, though many came grumbling, annoyed at being pulled from their meals or whatever leisure activity in which they were engaged. The younger men muttered about her "paranoia." But when the first figures appeared in the distance — dark-skinned wanderers with makeshift packs, their bodies lean but unbound — fear rippled through the ranks.

"Soldiers?" someone whispered.

"No... no uniforms..." another replied, uncertain.

The strangers walked cautiously, scanning the forest, until their eyes caught the faint smoke of the Kumakha fires. They froze. For a long, breathless moment, both groups stared at one another through the trees. Spears raised. Hearts thundered. The air cracked with the possibility of blood.

Edna stepped forward, ready to give the command to strike — when suddenly, one of the wanderers shrieked.

"Ghosts!" he cried, pointing wildly at the villagers emerging from behind the tree trunks. "The forest spirits live here! Run!"

Panic spread among the newcomers like fire in dry grass. Packs dropped, sandals kicked up dirt, and grown men and women sprinted headlong into the underbrush, tripping over roots and crashing through branches. Women screamed and scattered, children wailed, and the sight was so absurd that even the most stone-faced of Kumakha warriors could not hold their composure.

Laughter erupted, first a nervous chuckle, then a rolling thunder of hilarity. The younger villagers doubled over, clutching their sides. Even Joao's weary face broke into a grin. Edna herself allowed a smile, though her dagger remained lowered, cautious still.

When the frightened wanderers finally slowed, realizing the villagers were not pursuing them, a hesitant return began. This time, with less fear in their eyes. Words were exchanged, though incomprehensible, halting at first, and then substituted for signs, causing communication to flow freely as trust cautiously replaced suspicion.

And then the revelation came.

"We free," one of the men explained in clipped English, his voice shaking with the weight of history. "The Emancipation Act has passed. Slavery is over. We seek land. Land to buy, land to live as men and women, not property."

"I never thought the day would come when I would hear such words ... such sweet words," Edna said. Then she translated to her people.

The words struck them like thunder. For a long moment, silence reigned. Then gasps, whispers, tears. Nkechi clutched Edna's arm, her eyes wide with disbelief. Joao's staff slipped from his hand. Children looked up in confusion at their parents and grandparents'' trembling faces.

Slavery ... over? No overseers waiting beyond the trees? No chains, no ships, no soldiers with muskets ready to drag them back? The hiding, the drills, the fear — they were no longer necessary? The forest, which had so long been their prison and shield, seemed suddenly brighter, freer.

That night, the newcomers were welcomed into Kumakha village with open arms. Food was shared, stories exchanged, and for the first time in years, the laughter around the bonfire was not only of survival but of possibility.

When morning came, the newcomers made their choice. They purchased land on the western edge of the Kumakha and began to build. Their village rose slowly, with huts, gardens, and fires of their own. They named it Arkadea — a symbol, they said, of simplicity and untroubled happiness, a new life carved not from bondage and fear, but from choice.

And so, the Kumakhans were no longer alone. Two villages stood side by side: one born from resistance and vigilance, the other from newfound freedom. And though Edna's heart would never forget the price of blood, sweat, and tears, even she felt a weight lift from her shoulders. The world had changed. And now, so too would they.

THIRTEEN

The first months of Arkadea's founding were sweet with novelty. Neighbors exchanged food, helped one another build and mend huts, and cleared land side by side. But as the Arkadeans settled, old worlds clung to them like shadows. Many of the new arrivals carried the teachings of the missionaries who had hovered around the plantations like carrion birds. They brought with them Bibles, crosses carved from driftwood, and hymns sung in strange tongues. Around the Kumakha bonfires, where drums called forth the ancestors and voices lifted praises to Asase Yaa, the Arkadeans sometimes stood awkwardly at the edges, whispering disapproval.

"This ain't worship," one Arkadean woman muttered once, crossing herself. "It is obeah." The words spread, whispered again and again, until tension coiled between the two villages like a snake waiting to strike.

The Kumakha founding fathers and mothers, now elders bent but still fiery, resisted fiercely. They had fled the plantation not just to escape chains, but to preserve the spirits of their ancestors, their gods, their ways of living. To them, Christianity was a cloak for the whip, the overseer's mask. And they would not exchange their Kumakha drums for a European cross.

"You bow to dem god," Zinyanda spat, calling out an Arkadean woman with whom she had become friends, "but we bow only to de gods who bring us hey. The blood of Alkebula is not meant to kneel to Europe."

The Arkadeans bristled. Many were of mixed blood — children of violence and survival, their mothers Alkebulan, their fathers European or Amerindian or vice versa. To the Kumakhans, this was a mark of defilement. "Cursed blood," they whispered. "The children of both oppressor and oppressed — never whole, never pure."

The Arkadeans retaliated with words of their own. They began to call the Kumakhans *Jumbies*, forest ghosts clinging to a primitive way of life. Where the Kumakhans saw themselves as chosen, the Arkadeans saw superstition.

Inevitably, the two groups intermarried. Desire cares little for boundaries, and young men and women of both villages stole glances across fields, met at the banks of the canals, and shared laughter under the moon. When a Kumakhan

196

warrior's daughter bore a child with an Arkadean farmer, the fury of both communities flared.

"She has tainted her bloodline," the Kumakha elders lamented.

"They fear what they cannot change," the Arkadeans countered, proud of their mixed households.

And so, the two villages lived side by side for decades, bound by proximity yet divided by blood, faith, and the memory of chains. Festivals were separate, marriages often contested, children sometimes claimed by both and by neither.

But time is a river that wears down even the hardest stone.

Through generations, the Kumakhans and Arkadeans exchanged more than insults. They traded crops, exchanged medicines, borrowed techniques in farming, hunting, and craft. And slowly, the lines blurred. A Kumakhan boy reared by an Arkadean mother. An Arkadean child who danced to Kumakha drums. Mixed households multiplied until the very distinction began to fray.

Wars raged far away. Empires rose and fell. Colonies shifted hands. But under the canopy of the Kumakha tree, two peoples who had once seen each other as cursed and primitive, devil's spawn and jumbies, gradually softened into something new.

And then came the day — February 23, 1970.

By then, more than a century had passed since the first meeting. Guyana had declared itself a republic, severing the last chains of empire. On that day, beneath the same sky, Kumakhans and Arkadeans together lifted drums, crosses, songs, and dances. They paraded in costumes of every hue — habea leaves, feathers, beads, paint, and cloth — honoring not purity nor curse, but survival, resilience, and joy.

The festival was named Mashramani, "celebration after hard work." For the first time, the spirits of Kumakha and Arkadea danced together, not in opposition, but in unity. Drums mingled with tambourines. Dancers of mixed blood and pure blood spun side by side. Laughter replaced old insults. What had once nearly ended in bloodshed had transformed, through centuries of struggle, into a festival of rebirth.

And though Edna's bones had long since returned to the earth, those who still gathered beneath the Kumakha tree whispered her name. For it was her vigilance, her defiance, and her unyielding spirit that had made such a future possible.

FOURTEEN

By the late twentieth century, Edna the Warrior Princess was no longer just a memory passed around bonfires. She had become a legend, a name that carried the weight of myth, whispered by children in classrooms and invoked by elders in political speeches. To speak of Edna was to speak of defiance, of resilience, of a woman whose spirit had refused to bow.

Kumakha and Arkadea, once rival settlements bound in suspicion, were by then woven into the broader fabric of Guyana. Yet they retained an aura unlike any other community. To some, they were sacred sites, where freedom had taken its first fragile breath in the shadows of slavery. To others, they were curiosities, symbols of survival and syncretism. But for the emerging Black and Dougla middle class of the 1970s — teachers, artists, lawyers, musicians — they became something more: a cultural mecca.

The world itself was shifting. Across the Caribbean, Rastafari rhythm thundered, Pan-Africanism surged, and movements of Black Power swept young men and women into a tide of rediscovery. In Guyana, this awakening carried with it a hunger for roots deeper than empire, deeper than colonial classrooms. People wanted not just independence, but identity. It was in Kumakha and Arkadea that many found that sense of belonging, of connection.

The villages, side by side, bore living testimony to survival and transformation. Kumakha with its proud warrior lineages and ancestral rites. Arkadea with its stories of rebirth from bondage, its mixed families bridging the divides of blood. Together, they symbolized struggle and reconciliation.

Artists came first. Painters and poets, seeking inspiration from the Kumakha tree's towering presence. They sketched Edna as a goddess-warrior, dagger in hand, her eyes blazing against the colonial muskets. They wrote verses that wove her name with Asase Yaa, mother of the earth, protector of freedom.

Then came the families. Middle-class parents, swept by the spirit of Alkebulan pride, bought lands, and built homes, taking their children to festivals in the villages. They sought in Kumakha and Arkadea what the city could not give them: a place to reconnect with ancestral rhythm, with drumming circles and masquerade, with stories that had never bowed to Europe. Here, children learned to beat queh

queh drums, to dance the calinda, to speak words of Twi and Igbo and Yoruba carried faintly across the centuries.

Tensions did not vanish overnight. The scars of mistrust lingered, woven into old proverbs and guarded glances. Kumakhans still guarded their "purity" with pride. Arkadeans still remembered being called cursed. But time, culture, and the necessity of survival had braided their paths together. And Mashramani became the crown of that union.

Every February 23rd, the festival swelled into something larger than either village, larger even than the republic itself. Costumes burst with feathers, sequins, and cowrie shells; steelpan and drums pounded in unison; masqueraders embodied spirits both ancestral and new. And always, in the heart of the procession, someone carried Edna's likeness — a woman, young and fierce, holding a dagger aloft.

For the Black and Dougla middle class, this was more than spectacle. It was reclamation. It was a chance to rear their children not on shame but on pride, to root them not in colonial mimicry but in Alkebulan strength and glory. Kumakha and Arkadea became pilgrimage sites: villages that proved survival was not only possible, but transformative.

By the close of the twentieth century, Edna was no longer just a woman who had lived, fought, and bled. She was a heroine of the people, enshrined in Guyanese identity. Schools taught her story alongside that of Cuffy and Quamina. Artists painted her likeness on murals in Georgetown. During Mashramani, chants of her name rose above the music, threading past and present into one unbroken song.

And so, from a dagger raised in the forest to a festival bursting in the capital's streets, Edna's spirit endured. Not only as a memory, not only as folklore, but as the very heartbeat of a people who, even after centuries of chains and struggle, had found the strength to dance again — united under one sky.

PROLOGUE

The transatlantic slave trade was humanity's descent into its darkest cavern. For four centuries, millions of men, women, and children were torn from Alkebula, branded as cargo, and herded onto ships where disease, starvation, and despair claimed countless lives before they even touched foreign soil. Those who survived were chained to a lifetime of forced labor, their tongues beaten silent, their names erased, their gods mocked, their very humanity denied. The fields of the Americas, the Caribbean, and Europe's colonial empire were watered not just with sweat, but with the blood and tears of those who once stood free beneath the sun of their Motherland.

As a boy, when I first discovered the manuscript buried beneath the mound in our backyard, I relived vicariously the torment and triumph of Edna and her warrior clan. Through her eyes, I felt the iron biting flesh; through her spirit, I heard the muffled wails of mothers separated from children; through her heart, I endured the stench of flesh reduced to property. Yet with each page, I also witnessed something far greater than suffering: I saw defiance, I saw cunning, I saw endurance that refused to be broken.

Knowledge should have filled me with bitterness. By all logic, it should have ignited in me a hatred against those who chained, whipped, and commodified my people. But it did not. What Edna taught me, what her story revealed, was that hatred is too small a response to such an epic trial. Slavery was not the end of us. It was a passage — a crucible in the larger hero's journey of our people. It was the abyss we were forced to descend into, so that we might emerge bearing the true elixir: the knowledge of survival, the unyielding fire of freedom, and the sacred memory of those who refused to be erased.

It was in this light that I came to see her story not merely as an account of atrocity, but as the arc of redemption. For if the hero's journey demands death and resurrection, then slavery was the death forced upon us, and the generations that rose, free, unbroken, and still bearing the ancestral drumbeat in our veins, are the resurrection.

During the summer of 2025, I journeyed to Ghana to complete what the discovery of her manuscript had begun: the reconnection of her soul to the Motherland. In Sunyani, in the Ashanti Region not far from Kumasi, I felt her footsteps behind me. In Kumasi, I kissed the bare ground and felt the warmth of her matriarchal fire on my lips. On the third day, I traveled down to Cape Coast to visit that dungeon where the slave traders once packed our ancestors into darkness, shackled in their own blood, excrement, and tears, awaiting the ships that would cargo them across the Atlantic Ocean.

Standing in those cells on the fossilized waste of so many hopeless captives, breathing that air on which heavy suffering still lingered, I needed to invoke every ounce of Edna's spirit within me to endure the experience. For it is not easy to stand on the stones that drank one's ancestors' tears and maintain one's composure. Yet what struck me the most was the journey from Kumasi to Cape Coast itself: eight hours by car. My soul shuddered to even imagine Edna, ripped from her family, her people, her birthplace, walking that same distance with chains around her neck and ankles. That was a sobering revelation that shattered my heart and, at the same time, steeled my will. No matter how harsh the circumstances under which life may place me, I would never complain.

At the end of the passageway leading to the exit of the dungeon, the tour guide spoke words that will never leave me: "*Know that you carry in your veins the blood of some of the strongest, if not the strongest, people ever to walk the face of this earth. For only the strongest made it out that Door of No Return and across that ocean."*

In that moment, I felt not only Edna's presence, but the presence of all who had made it out and all who had perished. Finding the manuscript was no accident. It was an inheritance. A mandate. This is not merely the story of one woman, nor of one village, nor of one people. It is the saga of survival, of memory, of strength reborn in every generation. And I offer it now, with reverence and fire, so that you, too, may know her name, her struggle, her indomitable and unyielding spirit.

I am Michael Byrne, eleventh-generation descendant of Edna, the Warrior Queen of Kumakha.

ABOUT THE AUTHOR

George P A Dover is an author, publisher, language arts professor, spoken-word artist, and the CEO of Olai Multiversal Enterprises LLC and Global Elite Force Security, Inc. Over the years, he has earned many awards, including a Government of Guyana academic scholarship, a CMP Media Journalism Award, a Stony Brook Southampton College scholarship, and a joint scholastic editor award. His work spans newspapers, magazines, television, radio, and many internet platforms. He currently lives in Southern California with his lovely family.

www.ingramcontent.com/pod-product-compliance
Lightning Source LLC
Chambersburg PA
CBHW060143130626
46556CB00006B/2468